SIXTY-FOUR DEGREES

CHESLEY HINES

Wilderness settles peace on the soul because it needs no help;
it is beyond human contrivance.

From Edward O. Wilson, *The Diversity of Life*

authorHOUSE®

AuthorHouse™
1663 Liberty Drive
Bloomington, IN 47403
www.authorhouse.com
Phone: 1-800-839-8640

First published by AuthorHouse 6/10/2010

ISBN: 978-1-4490-7284-1 (e)
ISBN: 978-1-4490-7282-7 (sc)
ISBN: 978-1-4490-7283-4 (hc)

Library of Congress Control Number: 2010907896

Printed in the United States of America
Bloomington, Indiana

This book is printed on acid-free paper.

PART 1

SIXTY-FOUR NORTH

Have you gazed on naked grandeur where

There's nothing else to gaze on,

Set pieces and drop-curtain scenes galore,

Big mountains heaved to heaven, which the

Blinding sunsets blazon,

Black canyons where the rapids rip and roar?

Have you swept the visioned valley with the

green stream streaking through it,

Searched the Vastness for a something you have lost?

Have you strung your soul to silence?

Then for God`s sake go and do it;

Hear the challenge, learn the lesson, pay the cost.

From Robert Service, "The Call of the Wild"

August 2004

64°8' N, 141°2' W

A lone canoe glided through the softly falling snow and the mist rising from the Yukon River. Men were seated in the bow and stern of the canoe, and another man was lying amidships covered in a sleeping bag, with only his head visible. The men paddling were hunched over and looking down, though they occasionally glanced to each side to avoid looking into the snow. Their paddle strokes were weak. Fortunately, the river current was sufficient to propel them along. The Yukon River was rapidly freezing around them, but the ambient air was even colder, which created the mist rising from the water. Although the shore was not visible, the men apparently could see Eagle Bluff because the canoe turned to port toward the proximal shore fifty feet below the cliff overhanging the river, just upriver from the bluff. Had they not turned, they would have passed right by the hamlet of Eagle, Alaska, the last point of civilization, such as it is, before the Arctic Circle.

Ten days earlier, Thomas Speight McClamrock had stood on the banks of the Yukon River, gazing at the broad expanse of water beyond three heavily loaded canoes. The canoes were pulled up on the embankment just below the Front Street levee in Dawson City, Yukon, Canada.

As he studied the width of the river and the swiftly flowing current, he almost said out-loud, "I wonder if I have bitten off more than I can chew." As an experienced physician, he had instinctively learned to apply his medical assessment skills to everything in life, much like the famous Napoleon's Glance, the so-called coup d'oeil. For the first time, he realized that the Yukon was wider and swifter than the Mississippi at New Orleans. He rationalized that the Yukon was probably not as deep, and none of the whirlpools so typical of the Mississippi were visible. Nevertheless, he was concerned that he might have put his son Josh and himself in danger. It was too late to back out now, and he did not think his ego could bear the embarrassment of backing out anyway. Also, he genuinely wanted to make the trip with Josh, but he certainly did not want to endanger his son. So he tried to hide any concern by putting on an air of jocular bravado.

Tom was also disappointed in the Yukon's color and lack of clarity. He had assumed that the river would be clear, like a mountain stream. Instead, it looked milky, the result of it being a glacially fed river carrying detritus accumulated over hundreds of miles. Having grown up in Mississippi, where all the rivers and creeks were brown from muddy runoff, he had assumed that any stream in an area as pristine as he had imagined Alaska and northern Canada to be would certainly have clear rivers and streams.

"Where should we put the beer?" Josh asked.

This roused Tom out of his reverie. "Put two six-packs under each seat," Tom replied.

Instead of going to church, he and Josh had bought two six-packs of Yukon Gold and two of Arctic Red from a bar that Sunday morning. They had arrived in Dawson too late on Saturday afternoon to buy it from a grocery store, where it would have been much cheaper. Tom felt intensely guilty about not going to church, especially now that they were facing potential danger. Being a regular churchgoer, the thought of buying beer in a saloon on Sunday, directly at an

4

angle across the street from a church, was hard for him to handle. Although Tom was a Presbyterian, he still had a Mississippi Baptist guilt mentality, probably because his father had been a Baptist as a young man. Also, his mother was masterful at using guilt to control him. Nevertheless, he tried to justify it in his mind. They were about to leave, and he thought that having beer along would make the trip more enjoyable, especially since he wanted Josh to think that he was cool.

They had arrived in Dawson on the previous afternoon, along with their guide, Jim Grote, and a married couple, David and Diana Wortham, after an arduous journey from Eagle, Alaska. After an excellent night's sleep in a delightful bed-and- breakfast, and an outstanding and equally excellent breakfast of scrambled eggs, bacon, sausage, pancakes, and biscuits made from scratch, they were all in fine spirits.

Jim was a thirty-five-year-old history teacher in the Anchorage public school system. Of German and Russian ancestry, he was a native of North Dakota. He still said *ya* instead of yes, a reflection of his forebears. As one would expect from his northern European ancestry, Jim was blond, blue-eyed, and six feet tall, with rugged good looks and the lean and muscular build of a swimmer. He exuded confidence, and gave the appearance of being completely in control and comfortable in his role as a guide. He had been a guide on wilderness trips for many years, having worked in Utah, Colorado, and Montana before moving to Alaska. He was married, with one son, but his pregnant wife was due in one or two weeks. As was true of so many teachers, he could not make himself answer a question in a word or a sentence. It always took a paragraph or more to answer the most straightforward question. He realized this and would laugh at himself. If he didn't acknowledge this, Josh would quickly jump on it and make some quip like "Would you mind repeating that, Jim?"

The Worthams were from Manhattan, and were celebrating their eighth wedding anniversary. Diana was a psychiatric social worker, and David was the human resources manager for a utility company. They had met in the waiting room of a neurologist that they both were consulting—she for migraine headaches, and he for a seizure disorder. Diana was fifty years old and strikingly beautiful, with an almost perfect figure. She was not buxom. She was just perfectly proportioned for her five-foot seven-inch frame. There was a seductiveness in her mannerisms that was hard to describe. Tom found it distasteful, because it was so blatant and obvious. Josh thought it was beguiling, attractive, and downright sexy.

David was fifty-two years old, lean but not muscular, and approximately five feet five inches tall, by Tom's estimation. He clearly was shorter than Diana. Josh called him a nerd. He had an aggravating habit of asking Jim the same question that had just been answered five minutes earlier, either because of a hearing problem or due to preoccupation. In addition, while listening to the answer to his question, he would keep his mouth open so long that Josh told Tom that it was remarkable he did not swallow bugs.

Alaska-Yukon Adventure Tours had arranged for the little group to spend the night in a bed-and-breakfast in Anchorage before starting the trip to the Yukon River. The next morning, Jim had picked up the four guests in the company van. There were two bucket seats up front and two bench seats in back, the one closer to the front being shorter than the one in the far rear because of the step on the right side of the van.

Diana sat in the front bucket seat all the way from Anchorage to Eagle. Josh and Tom sat on the bench seat behind Jim and Diana, and David sat on the far back bench seat by himself. Diana talked incessantly to Jim, stopping only when she dozed off from time to time. She often asked him very personal questions about the girlfriends he had dated before he met his wife.

Josh asked Tom during a gas stop, "Can you believe that she asked him how he satisfied his sexual needs while on these wilderness trips?"

Tom tried to rationalize this question by replying, "This may be the type of question that she might ask one of her patients. Remember that she is a psychiatric social worker."

It struck Josh and Tom as rather odd that a couple on their wedding anniversary did not sit together.

Their first campsite on the road trip from Anchorage to Eagle was at the base of the Gulkana Glacier, about a half-mile downstream from the terminal moraine on the bank of a roaring stream created by melting ice. Tom climbed up on top of the van to help Jim pass down the gear to Josh and David.

While up there, Tom said, "Jim, I'm sorry, but I don't see the glacier."

"It's that dark wall up the stream," Jim replied.

"That ugly thing?" said Tom.

"Yes, I'm afraid so."

"I always thought that glaciers were white, white like a bar of Ivory soap," Tom said, the disappointment obvious in his voice.

The moraine was indeed ugly, the ice of the glacier being covered in a layer of ground up rocks from its centuries old migration down the mountain valley above it. Tom thought that the dark gray color of the oncoming moraine made it look foreboding and threatening, almost evil.

When the gear had been unloaded, Jim said, "While we're setting up camp, let me tell you a little bit about glaciers. Rock material eroded by mountain glaciers and ice sheets is called till, and consists of particles that range from tiny fragments to boulders. This detritus is carried downhill by the glacier, and then deposited over surrounding landscapes. Till that is deposited at the sides of glaciers is known as a lateral moraine, and creates ridges parallel to ice flow.

On a grander scale, the lateral moraine created by one or more of the glaciers that covered the northern part of North America as recently as eleven thousand years ago is exemplified by Long Island, Block Island, the Elizabeth Islands in Buzzards Bay, Martha's Vineyard, Nantucket, and Cape Cod. If two glaciers merge, a medial moraine is formed from the till, while ridges formed at right angles to the front edge of a glacier are called terminal moraines. The glacier up the little stream above us is a classic example of one with a terminal moraine. By the way, you will find that I am obsessed with glaciers, so, if you get tired of hearing about them, let me know."

"This glacier is strikingly different from the Bear Glacier, which Josh and I saw from Resurrection Bay when we were fishing for silver salmon before this trip," Tom said.

"That's true," Jim replied. "Bear Glacier is one of many glaciers that are an extension of the Harding Icefield, which covers more than half of the Kenai Fjords National Park. As the four of you flew into Anchorage, if the weather was not cloudy, you probably had the opportunity to view that enormous ice field. It gave you a glimpse back to when ice covered much of North America, since the glaciers in the far north of North America are the vestiges of that ice sheet which formed 2.6 million years ago, and retreated as recently as ten thousand years ago. As opposed to the Gulkana Glacier, Bear Glacier has a medial moraine, with a branch of the glacier on each side of the moraine. The glacier then abruptly ends its journey by dropping off large and small chunks of ice into Resurrection Bay."

To reach the Gulkana glacier above their campsite, they had to hike up the boulder-strewn riverbed below it. The boulders were either spherical, about the size of pomegranates, or oblate, about the size of grapefruits. As the group stumbled along, Jim said, "Let me point out here that these rounded, smooth rocks have been shaped that way by centuries of grinding by the heavy glacier above them. As the glacier melted, it receded and left the rocks behind. The fields and forests of New England show the same deposition of boulders that were left by the receding North American ice sheet."

There was no way to walk around the boulders. The group had to walk on top of them. Diane and David could not keep up with Jim, Josh, and Tom, partly because they were not wearing boots, and partly because they had not prepared themselves physically for this kind of outing. The brochure from Alaska-Yukon Adventure Tours had laid out a detailed program of fitness necessary for them to follow in preparation for the trip. The McClamrocks had followed the instructions precisely, but the Worthams had ignored the recommendations as to physical preparation, and proper clothing and footwear.

And then they reached a swinging footbridge that crossed the roaring little river below. They had to cross the bridge to reach the terminal moraine of the glacier. The bridge was intimidating to everyone except for Josh, who, like typical young men, thought he was invincible. By the time everyone had crossed the bridge, darkness was descending rapidly.

Tom grumbled to Josh, "If Diane and David had not insisted on reading every damn written word at the Iditarod Museum earlier in the day, we would have arrived at the campsite an hour earlier."

Now, in the Arctic twilight, they turned around and stumbled back toward camp over the boulders. Diana twisted her ankle when her foot slid down the side of one of the boulders, so quickly that it was like stepping on icy pavement. Josh carried her back to her tent, with her riding piggyback on his back, while Jim and Tom went ahead to prepare an ice-bag for her ankle. They all reached their tents just before a major thunderstorm swept in. Diana went to sleep with the ice pack on her ankle, and she awoke the next morning free of any pain or swelling.

As they packed up their gear, Josh asked Tom, "How'd you sleep last night, Dad?"

"Fine, how about you?" replied Tom.

"I'm glad," said Josh, "I remember that you said that you would never put your body on the ground again, after Viet Nam."

"That's true, but I've eaten crow before."

In Eagle, they picked up their canoes, along with paddles, life jackets, and knee boots. The canoes were strapped securely to a trailer, which was then hooked up to the van. Their duffle bags and backpacks were secured to a rack on top of the van. They would be returning back to Eagle via the Yukon River in a few days. The owner of Alaska-Yukon Adventure Tours, Rusty Shaw, had flown in to Eagle in his four-seat Cessna. He was to join them on the trip to Dawson to bring the van back to Eagle, since Jim would need a vehicle to bring the guests back to Anchorage after their canoe trip down the river.

Rusty spent the night in a cabin that his tour company owned. The cabin had been occupied in 1904 by the famous Norwegian explorer Roald Amundsen. The group ate hamburgers in the cabin that night. Tom and Josh stayed in one of the cabins adjoining the Amundsen cabin. Amundsen was the latest in a long line of explorers that had fascinated Tom. He couldn't believe that they were actually seeing Amundsen's cabin.

He excitedly told Josh, "Amundsen is best known as the first person to reach the South Pole. However, prior to that feat, he sailed from Norway through the Arctic Circle and discovered the long-sought Northwest Passage to the Pacific. Due to global warming, cargo vessels can now ply the Northwest Passage between northern Europe and Asia, but one hundred years ago, the Arctic Ocean would freeze solid during the winter. He and his five-man crew spent two winters frozen into the Arctic ice, sailing during the summer months in a single-masted sloop not much bigger than ours. During that time they learned survival skills from the Eskimos, such as how to make the skis faster, how to use animal skins for better protection against the bitter cold (caribou hair is hollow and thus creates an insulation), and how to make igloos. These skills were later instrumental in helping Amundsen and his companions reach the South Pole. When he reached Herschel Island on the Arctic coast of the Yukon Territory, he and three other men walked, skied, snowshoed, and dog-sledded for five hundred miles to reach the telegraph station at Fort Egbert, on the edge of Eagle, to let his friends and family in Norway, and the rest of the world, know that he had discovered the Northwest Passage and was alive."

Over dinner that night, Rusty said, "Let me tell you a little bit about Eagle, Alaska. In the gold rush days of 1898, Eagle had as many as twenty thousand inhabitants, but now there are only one hundred eighty-five year-round residents. There is a ranger station on the grounds of Fort Egbert, a restaurant, a service station, a post office, a small motel, and thirty or forty cabins and houses. We feel very fortunate to own one of the cabins, especially such an historic one. In the days of Eagle's prominence, there was a U.S. Army base here. It was commanded by a Lieutenant William Mitchell, who later became the famous General Billy Mitchell. He's considered the father of the U.S. Air Force. He was court-martialed on questionable grounds. Lieutenant Mitchell and his men established the first telegraph line from Alaska back to the mainland of the United States, and they did it in the dead of winter. Amundsen was aware of this, and that is why he chose to make the five-hundred-mile trek from the Arctic Ocean."

Rusty had arranged for the group to take a tour of historic Eagle. After a preliminary lecture by the tour guide, it was apparent to Tom and Josh that Tom knew more about Amundsen than the guide. When they began the tour of the old cabins, Tom and Josh quietly slipped away and wandered around the village on their own tour. They went to the ranger station, which was not on the guided tour. They picked up some interesting brochures and bought a copy of the *Yukon River Guide*, which provided interesting facts about the river from Dawson to Eagle.

Josh was especially fascinated by a kennel of dogs that were a mixture of the Siberian and Alaskan husky breeds. He said, "Dad, did you hear that? That husky sounded exactly like a wolf." In fact, the huskies looked just like wolves to Tom.

As they continued their sojourn in Eagle, they found two old settlers sitting on a bench outside a small grocery store. Tom and Josh were particularly amused by a heavily bearded man with a pistol in a holster attached to his belt. His pants were so low that as he leaned across a table the crack between his buttocks was visible. Tom pulled out his camera to take a photograph of the man and his buttocks, but Josh quietly whispered, "Dad, I'm not sure that I would do that. He has a pistol." Tom remembered seeing a sign on a nearby roof that proudly said, "States' Rights." Considering all of this, he decided that taking a photograph of the man would be ill advised. Meanwhile, the Worthams painstakingly went through every historical cabin in the village and read every placard, thus delaying the departure to Dawson until the afternoon.

Tom said to Josh, "I think I'm going to have to cool my jets because it is obvious that the Worthams are going to do exactly what they want to do, with no thought of the wishes of the others in the group."

From Eagle, the group had ridden one hundred sixty miles to the southeast on the Taylor Highway, which was basically a glorified logging road, to where it joined the Top of the World Highway at Chicken, which had a population of only seventeen residents. As they stopped to fill up with gas and use the restrooms, Jim said, "The gold miners in the area had wanted to name this town for the native ptarmigan, but they could not spell ptarmigan; so they named the town chicken."

Josh thought that was a wonderful story. As he dashed into the service station store he said, "I've got to get a T-shirt or a cap that says Chicken on it." He promptly came out with a cap that had Chicken, Alaska, on the front. He said, "I told the woman inside that I had come all the way from New Orleans to get a cap from Chicken."

"You're a mess," said Tom, laughing as he usually did at his son's sense of humor.

The road from Eagle to Chicken had been a steady climb through beautiful mountain valleys, along rushing streams feeding into the Fortymile River. Because the road from Eagle was unpaved, getting behind another vehicle or passing another vehicle meant that the van would fill with dust. In addition, there were several small forest fires very near the edge of the road, the smoke from which was always permeating the van.

While passing across a high plateau, surrounded by low mountains, Jim suddenly slammed on the brakes, and said, "Bear!" A large grizzly was chasing a young moose up the mountainside on the left side of the van at a speed that must have been thirty miles an hour. The two animals passed out of sight over the crest of the mountain.

Tom and Josh excitedly jumped out of the van with their binoculars to try to see the two animals better. Jim got out to try to help them find them in their binocular sights, but they were long gone. David and Diana stayed in the van, apparently somewhat bored with the whole spectacle.

At another point on the road, Jim suddenly stopped the van. In a marshy meadow on the right side of the highway, a lone caribou buck was lazily grazing in the tall grass that came up to his chest.

"Wow, what a magnificent rack of antlers," Tom said in quiet awe.

"Why isn't he with a herd?" Josh asked.

"I really don't know why," Jim replied. "It really doesn't make sense, since caribou usually travel in a herd."

On the other side of the road, in a marshy lake area, there were literally thousands of ducks. Tom and Josh had been avid duck hunters until the dues at Tom's duck club became prohibitively expensive, and Tom was compelled to resign. Those days of duck hunting together had been some of the best days of their lives. Two subsequent retinal separations in Tom's eyes had reinforced his decision. Now, gazing down on the massive flight of ducks, Tom said, "Josh, can you believe the long journey south facing them? I wonder if any of these ducks will end up in the rice fields and marshes and swamps of Louisiana, and, maybe, in some of our friends' duck gumbo."

The Top of the World Highway was mostly paved and ran along the top of a high ridge between forty-five hundred and five thousand feet above sea level, until it reached the Yukon River, some sixty miles away. The group could easily understand why it was named the Top of the World Highway. At the U.S. and Canadian border, everyone in the van was thoroughly interrogated in a polite manner, and then sent on their way into the Yukon Territory. Finally, they descended down a very steep slope to an overlook high above the western shore of the mighty Yukon, where the town of Dawson could be seen directly across the river.

"Okay, let's get out of the van here, so I can give you another one of my lectures," Jim said.

While the four tour guests gazed at the spectacular view of their destination after the long, tiresome ride in the van, Jim pronounced in his best schoolteacher voice, "The Gwich'in people of the Athabascan Native Americans, who inhabit the lower portions of the Yukon River, called it the *Yuk-un-ah*, meaning great river. And it is a great river—all nineteen hundred twenty miles of it. The Yukon is the longest river in Alaska, and the third longest in the United States. Beginning as a small stream in British Columbia only fifteen miles from the Pacific Ocean, it heads northwest to the Arctic Circle, and then it makes an abrupt ninety-degree turn to the southwest toward the Bering Sea. In the meantime, it drains half of Alaska, three-quarters of the Yukon Territory, and parts of British Columbia. The southern edge of the town you're looking at is bordered by the clear little Klondike River, the site of the famous gold strike that precipitated the famous gold rush of 1896."

"Hey, you can see it to our right," Josh exclaimed. The clear water of the Klondike was in striking contrast to the muddy Yukon.

"Josh is right. Do you all see it?" Jim asked. "Okay, let's get back in the van and go down to the ferry landing."

A primitive ferry carried them across the rapidly flowing river to the landing at Dawson. Then Jim drove the van to a bed-and-breakfast located one block from the well-preserved cabin of Jack London, the author of so many stories about the Yukon and the gold rush, the most well-known being *The Call of the Wild*. After they had dropped off their gear, Jim gathered everyone together. "Let's take a walk around Dawson, so I can tell you some things about it," he said.

Rusty had ridden with them in the van to take it back to Eagle, so that it would be available when the canoeists returned. Jim asked him, "Rusty, would you mind coming along, in case I forget something?"

"Sure, I'd be happy to."

Jim began, "The town of Dawson has been preserved essentially as it was one hundred years ago. The streets are unpaved and the sidewalks are wooden, since the freezing weather in the winter would destroy concrete and asphalt. Dawson has eighteen hundred year-round residents, but, during the gold rush that happened around the turn of the twentieth century, the population swelled to approximately thirty thousand. After the California gold rush in 1849, prospectors began to search for gold all over the Pacific Northwest of the United States, as well as in Alaska and the Yukon

Territory of Canada. These men were called sourdoughs because they lived off the land, and they carried a rucksack containing a gold pan, a pick, shovel, beans, bacon, tea, and a crock of fermented dough, which was called sourdough.

"In August 1896, one sourdough working alone, and three others who were working together discovered gold in creeks feeding into the Klondike River. Abiding by the sourdough unwritten code of conduct, they shared this information with other prospectors in the region. When the prospectors who were living and working in the towns of Fortymile, Yukon, and Circle City, Alaska, heard about the gold strike, they abandoned the two settlements and moved upriver to Dawson. By the summer of 1897, there were twenty-five hundred people living in tents in Dawson. Primitive cabins subsequently replaced the tents. Some of those cabins have been preserved, such as the ones Robert Service and Jack London once owned. There are also classic western-style saloons with rooms for rent on the second and third floors. During the winter of 1897–98 roughly one million people made plans to go to the Klondike gold fields. About one hundred thousand actually started out; about forty thousand reached the gold fields by the summer of 1898. Have I left out anything, Rusty?"

"You're doing fine, Jim," Rusty replied.

"The journey from San Francisco, Seattle, Portland, or Vancouver to Dawson was a formidable one. The all-water route was the safest way and required the least amount of work, but it was also the most expensive. The first leg was twenty-seven hundred fifty miles by ocean steamer to the mouth of the Yukon River, where it empties into the Bering Sea. From there, passengers transferred to river steamers, or paddle wheelers, for the seventeen hundred miles up the Yukon to Dawson.

"Most of the stampeders, as they were often called, chose to go by ship through the Inside Passage to Skagway or Dyea, and then hike over either the White Pass or the Chilkoot Pass. The hardships of carrying themselves and their supplies over these passes were unbelievable. Then, if and when they made it over the passes, they had to build primitive boats to take them and their supplies down the wild Yukon River to Dawson. When the Yukon froze, dogsleds were used to bring the mail and vital supplies such as medicine over these two passes and down the frozen river to Dawson."

Rusty interjected, "These trips are eloquently described in Jack London's classic story, *The Call of the Wild.*"

"Good point," said Jim.

The four guests seemed to be spellbound by the story, not saying a word or asking a single question. Not even David asked any questions, which surprised Tom and Josh.

Just before dusk and after the tour group had broken up prior to meeting for dinner, Tom and Josh found a gold shop where the lady proprietor was a descendant of the owners of the original Fortymile gold mine. The mine was famous because it marked the site of the first gold strike in the Yukon Territory, and it happened several years before the Klondike discovery. Members of her family were still mining the Fortymile strike. Her shop was filled with magnificent mammoth tusks that were uncovered in the process of mining for gold. The tusks had been preserved for ten thousand years because they were buried in the permafrost. With her assistance, Tom and Josh designed a pendant-brooch from a gold nugget to be shipped to Mom back home in New Orleans.

After a dinner of halibut and several glasses of Yukon Gold and Arctic Red beer at Klondike Kate's Restaurant, Josh, Tom, Jim, and Rusty ended the evening at the Sourdough Saloon. The Worthams did not drink alcohol, she because of her migraines and he because of his seizure disorder. They went back to the bed-and-breakfast. At the saloon, Tom and Josh became members of the Sourtoe Club, which entailed drinking a shot of Yukon Jack containing the big toe of an old miner who had lost his toe due to frostbite. They had to touch the toe with their lips to be accepted into this "elite" society. They passed the entrance requirements, but they were rather appalled the next morning at what they had done. They were also proud. Being a member of the Sourtoe Club was not exactly the same as being a member of a Carnival organization in New Orleans. Nevertheless, for posterity, there were videos taken of each of them quaffing a glass of Yukon Jack, and touching the toe against their lips.

At the levee the next morning, Josh said, "Dad, I can't believe that I feel this good after all the drinking we did last night."

"That stack of pancakes with maple syrup probably replaced all the glycogen in your liver that had been lost because of the alcohol. You remember glycogen from chemistry, don't you?"

"Actually, I do, believe it or not."

Rusty had dropped off the three canoes, and then headed back to Eagle with the van and the empty trailer, leaving the five of them on the levee landing with their canoes and gear. Jim had directed the loading of the canoes with the food, tents, stove, ice chests, ten gallon-size plastic water bottles, and personal gear in such a way that the canoes were balanced. However, perceiving the differences in strengths of the various members of the group, he directed that the heavier items be placed in his canoe and the McClamrock canoe.

"Everybody ready?" Jim asked as he checked to make sure that everyone had his or her life vests on. "Remember to paddle on opposite sides of the canoe. The power comes from the paddler in the bow. The person in the stern is mainly responsible for maintaining the direction of the canoe. The river current is running at twelve to fifteen miles per hour, so no one should have to work very hard. If someone capsizes, everyone should first come to the rescue of the people in the water. After that is done worry about retrieving the spilled items, and, lastly, worry about retrieving the canoe. Any questions? Okay, let's go."

Dead silence. The apprehension was palpable. Slowly, they pushed the three canoes off from the shore, the canoes rocking frightfully until the paddlers could get their balance. The gunwales were low in the water with the heavy loads of equipment and supplies, and, of course, the paddlers themselves. As they headed out into the current, Tom was in awe of how small the canoes appeared to be in the mighty river.

Jim turned his canoe broadside to the other canoes, and said, "The river carries with it millions of tons of silt from the glaciated ranges of Alaska and Canada, so much so that the silt can actually be heard scraping the bottom of the canoes as the canoes pass through the water. Do you hear it?"

"Yes, yes, I do," exclaimed Diana.

"Wait until the ferry gets halfway across the river, and then paddle like mad to get below its path before it returns," Jim yelled. Since they had crossed the river on the ferry in the van on the previous afternoon, they knew that the ferry moved rapidly across the river, and, consequently, they didn't have much time to get beyond the path of the ferry. Tom was actually more worried that the wake of the ferry might swamp the canoes than the ferry hitting the canoes. David and Diana pulled their canoe as closely behind Jim's as possible without bumping into his canoe. As Tom followed behind them with Josh, he could sense that they were tense. The canoes passed the path of the ferry quickly.

Jim announced, "Very soon we will be slipping by the ancient Han village. The Han were a branch of the Athabascan nation that lived in the section of the river between Dawson and Eagle. Han is a Gwich'in word meaning people of the river."

Tom was struck by the fact that there was also an ancient Chinese Han Dynasty, and that the ancestors of these inhabitants had come across the land bridge between Asia and North America about twenty thousand years ago.

Could they be the same people? Tom wondered.

Jim turned his canoe to the right again and said, "The Gwich'in were a migratory people who inhabited that village over there. They hunted muskrats, beavers, ducks, geese, moose, caribou, rabbits, and grouse, and they fished for whitefish and salmon."

The group then stopped to explore a steamship graveyard on the shore on the left side of the river. As they wandered around through the iron debris scattered in various locations, Jim explained, "The sternwheelers that plied the Yukon during the gold rush were the same as those that had been used on the Mississippi River and its tributaries, such as the Yazoo River, in the 1800s."

"We still have sternwheelers in New Orleans that are used to take tourists up and down the Mississippi," Josh said.

"Interesting," Jim replied.

The weather was warm and sunny, and before Diana got back in her canoe, she took off her shirt and long pants, leaving her clad in short-shorts and a halter top. Although the three men who were not married to her tried not to look at her, they could not refrain from doing so. David did not appear to acknowledge her.

As they pulled away from the steamboat graveyard, Jim turned to face the others and said, "If you will look on the other side of the river, you will see the site of old Fort Reliance, a trading post established in 1874 to deal with the Han Indians. Fort Reliance was abandoned in 1877 after the Native Americans stole the traders' goods. The wood from the abandoned buildings was later used as fuel for the steamboats that plied the Yukon during the gold rush."

Then they were all alone on the vast river, one hundred five miles from their destination—Eagle, Alaska. The quietness was palpable, though the soft squishing sound of the paddles entering the water broke the silence. There was also the faint grinding sound of the tiny particles in the water as they rubbed against the metal canoes passing down the river.

Canoeing the Yukon River had been a dream of Tom's for more than ten years. Now it was coming true. At sixty-four, he knew that he had to make a trip like this before he got older, before the age-related risks of heart disease and stroke caught up with him. He had been exercising regularly and intensely for a year in preparation for the trip, and he felt that he was in excellent physical condition. He still stood erectly, at five feet eleven inches, as if he were still in the military service. He did not feel old in any way. (When he was younger, he was six feet tall. He would tell people that he had lost an inch because he was married to a short woman.) Tom had wondered to himself why he wanted to make this trip. After all, he was a respected physician, both locally and nationally, he had a good marriage and two fine children, and he was a proper member of most of the correct social establishments of New Orleans. He wondered, *What has made me want to make this trip so badly? Am I trying to prove something to myself or about myself?*

Tom had never been an athlete. This had always left him feeling somewhat inadequate, although he was reasonably good at the four hundred forty-yard dash in track. In high school, the most admired boys were football stars. Tom's vision was so bad that he could not see the football unless it was three feet from him. His high school years preceded the development of comfortable contact lenses; what a difference ten years might have made. He had the same problem with softball and baseball, often being hit in the forehead by the oncoming ball. He did enjoy outdoor activities, such as duck hunting, fishing, hiking, and, obviously, canoeing as well as kayaking. Tom had always loved to have a little adventure in his life, even though he did not consider himself to be particularly courageous. As he paddled, he thought about his life, and why he might have wanted to make the trip.

In spite of his self-perceived lack of courage, Tom had found himself in several situations as a young man that had required considerable courage. He had worked in Colombia on an epidemiological research project funded by the National Institutes of Health between his second and third year in medical school. It was the beginning of the insurgency in Colombia, by what was then called the *Violencia*. These bands of guerilla-bandits later formed the Cali Cartel and the Medellin Cartel, so important in the trafficking of cocaine to the United States and elsewhere. The experience made him realize that he could survive and actually thrive in a foreign land.

Between his third and fourth year in medical school, Tom received a fellowship to work in a Presbyterian mission hospital in the Republic of the Congo. Malaria and sleeping sickness were rampant, as well as other infectious diseases. During that summer, his physician/patron and he went crocodile hunting at night on the Kasai River, a river brimming with crocodiles and hippopotami. The Simba Revolution in the Congo took place that summer of 1964. After two and a half months in Africa, he left, upon the insistence of the U.S. State Department. This experience reinforced his awareness that he could handle himself in exotic environments and enjoy the experience. This also made him aware that he really loved adventure.

After finishing his internship, he had spent a year in Vietnam. As an Air Force physician assigned to an Army forward compound, he was asked to take command of a bunker during the Tet Offensive of 1968. He was awarded the Bronze Star. His main duties were helping the one remaining Vietnamese physician to take care of the civilians, but the compound was so small that everyone participated in guard duty at night. The Viet Cong often launched mortar attacks at night, and there was also small arms fire. Trips to the bunkers were consequently frequent. At the civilian hospital, Tom had the opportunity to treat malaria, plague, cholera, snakebites, tetanus, rabies, and intestinal parasites. These were diseases that, for the most part, he had only read about in medical school, and he never dreamed that he would actually encounter them in his work. Thus, it was an enriching experience and one that he cherished.

Josh had had less experience in a canoe, but he had already become a skilled canoeist. Tom surmised that Josh had come along on the trip partly to take care of his old man. He was twenty-two years old, and a senior at Tulane University in New Orleans. He was ruggedly handsome at five feet ten inches tall, with dark hair and bright, pale blue eyes. He was in superb physical condition. Tom knew that Josh was extremely intelligent, although his grades did not reflect it unless he was intensely interested in the subject. In Tom's opinion, Josh was very clever and witty, and he had Tom's penchant for learning minutiae that might be worthless, except for the fun of knowing the information.

It was already autumn in the Yukon. The scene reminded Tom of the Big Two Hearted River in the Upper Peninsula of Michigan, and the headwaters of the Kennebec and Penobscot Rivers of Maine. The aspen and birch leaves were bright yellow, and the trees were nestled in the protected bends of the river on the lower portions of the low mountains. On the more exposed sections of the mountains, the spruce trees were dark green. When the aspens and the birches were adjacent to the spruces, the color contrasts were stunningly beautiful. Native Americans once used birch trees like the ones Tom and Josh were admiring to make birch-bark canoes. When French explorers first arrived in Canada, the native people taught them how to make and paddle the canoes.

On the higher reaches of the mountains, there was only tundra because of the permafrost, the condition where the ground never thaws below the top eighteen to twenty-four inches. Trees are unable to establish root systems in the permafrost, which accounted for the tundra grass. Much of the river edge was sheer cliffs of gray granite, slate, and shale interspersed with red layers of iron ore and occasional yellow quartz. Tom thought to himself, bemusedly, *These layers of rocks remind me of Napoleons, my favorite dessert.* Where there had been a shift in the rock layers, it was almost as if someone had cut the Napoleon with a fork.

Jim turned his canoe so that he could face the four guests and said, "These rock formations are the oldest rocks in the Alaska-Yukon area, between six hundred and eight hundred million years old. Until two hundred million years ago, this area was ocean. Around that time, through plate tectonics, these rocks were deposited along the western margin of North America, where the Yukon River now lies."

"Very interesting," David said in one of his rare moments of speaking.

Jim paddled the lead canoe. It carried the stove and the two propane tanks for fuel, and the perishable food in an Igloo ice chest. He also had his tent and personal items, such as a change of clothes and a sleeping bag.

Following Jim were the Worthams. They obviously had had little or no experience with canoeing. Diana made little dipping motions with her paddle, but never put any real effort into pulling backward with the paddle stroke. David spent most of the time using the paddle as a rudder, instead of using any strength that he might possess to pull the canoe forward downstream. Their canoe contained some of the lighter, more perishable food items, such as bread. They also carried their tent, clothes, and sleeping bags.

Fortunately, Jim had loaded a great deal of the heavier items in either his canoe or in the canoe paddled by Josh and Tom. The McClamrock canoe carried two large plastic containers of water, plus their personal items, tent, and sleeping bags. The father and son team had volunteered to bring up the rear of the little flotilla, in case the canoe paddled by the Worthams capsized. Each canoe was equipped with a rescue rope to be used in the possibility of such a mishap.

It was a beautiful warm sunny Sunday afternoon. As the five paddlers settled down into a rhythm with the river current, it almost seemed like they were paddling along in time with one of

Puccini's sweeping majestic melodies, and that the canoes were dancers moving along and across the grand ballroom, which was the Yukon River, waltzing from one side of the river to the other to keep on the outside of the curves, which allowed them to stay in the swifter current and avoid running aground on a sandbar. Rivers possess this almost animalistic desire to wander or, by definition, to meander. They erode the banks of one side along their course, and then deposit sediments from the eroded bank on the opposite side, and so it goes inexorably back and forth down the path of the river.

When they reached the Twelve Mile River, so named because it was twelve miles downriver from old Fort Reliance, Jim pulled over to shore and shouted back to the others, "Let's stop here and make camp." The sandbar adjacent to the pristine little river was a perfect spot for the tents. The sound of the rapids in the Twelve-Mile River would rock them to sleep.

Tom quietly said to Jim, "Aren't you concerned by the number of bear, wolf, and moose tracks in the sand?" But Jim was unconcerned. "There are that many tracks on every sandbar on the river. We just have to keep the food out of sight and out of scent."

"Okay." Tom said as he nodded in acceptance.

Setting up camp was the first priority of the Worthams and the McClamrocks, while Jim began to set up the field kitchen, with its propane stove and aluminum folding table for food preparation and serving. Tom and Josh learned quickly to put three or four bottles of beer in a mesh bag, and then hang the bag over the stern of the beached canoe. By the time the camp was ready, the beer would be properly chilled. Before the tents could be erected, suitable space on the sandbar had to be cleared of boulders. The tents were three-person tents with waterproof floors. Since only two people were assigned to each one, the tents could easily contain the dry bags of clothes and other items without crowding the campers. Josh had had experience in setting up tents like these while on a wilderness hike in Oregon and Washington when he was thirteen years old. Therefore, he became very useful around the campsite.

"While you finish nailing down the tent stays, I'm going to go help the Worthams, Okay?" Josh announced to Tom.

"Sure. I've got this under control."

"Don't you think that you are putting your tent awfully close to the bushes, David?" Josh asked.

"No, we want to hear the river."

"Okay," Josh said.

Josh and Tom wanted to stay away from any vegetation to avoid any wandering wildlife that might hide in it, so they pitched their tent near the shore of the Yukon. Jim placed his tent closer to the kitchen area, and he began to set up the portable table and stove. The actual kitchen area was separated from the tents by fifteen to twenty yards to avoid attracting bears to the tent area.

Josh said, "Let's go explore the upstream portion of this pretty little river."

Tom replied, "I'm concerned about what we might encounter, since this looks like a natural habitat for moose. Moose love marshy areas where there is tender vegetation for them to eat. Even though moose are rather stupid creatures and have poor eyesight, they are huge, and the bulls have enormous antlers. When surprised, they are prone to charge. A cow with a calf is equally formidable. In fact, moose are a constant threat on the highways of Maine. Whenever a highway passes through a valley where there is a bog, there will be a road sign advising drivers of the possibility of moose crossing the highway."

Nevertheless, Tom reluctantly agreed to go along on the exploration.

David Wortham asked, "Do you two mind if I tag along, too? Diana has requested some private time to clean up before dinner."

"Of course, you can come with us," Josh said.

As they started off, Jim advised, "Keep a sharp eye out for bears and moose." They had already discovered some large bear tracks in the sand at the campsite, so they were aware that bears were in the area.

Tom then asked David, "Are you sure that you want to go?"

"Yes, I need to get away from my wife for a while."

"Okay, let's go, but everybody watch out for bears and moose," Tom said.

The three of them tried to cross the Twelve Mile River near the Wortham tent, but there was a deep pool there. They noticed several fifteen- to twenty- inch trout in the pool.

"Damn, Josh! We should have brought our fishing gear," Tom declared.

Josh said, "They must be rainbow trout, since steelhead, brook trout, and brown trout do not live in the Yukon watershed."

"How'd you know that?" David asked.

"Just one of my tidbits of information that I like to keep around."

A few yards below the pool, the little river widened and became shallow, allowing an easier crossing. Upstream, the river turned to the left and divided around an island. The three men, or rather, Josh, elected to take the channel closer toward the mountains, with Tom and David following him, and then the camp was out of sight. They slogged on up the progressively shallower river as quietly as they could, not talking and trying to avoid splashing water like three little boys on a scavenger hunt. They hiked through a marshy area that was clearly moose country. They were fully aware that a charging moose could be deadly, but they were still hoping to see one.

Diana had watched the three of them until they passed out of sight. Noting that they were beyond the sight of camp and that Jim was around the other side of the bushes, tending to preparation of dinner, she decided that this would be an opportune time to bathe in the deep pool. Taking off all her clothes, she timidly put her bare feet into the frigid water. She was shocked at how cold it was. She decided that she could stand the water temperature for a few seconds. She then submerged her entire body and her head into the water, but she shot up immediately with the shock to her body. Since she had gone that far, she made herself lather her hair with shampoo, and she used the frothy shampoo to bathe her body. She then contemplated the cold water again. Knowing that she had to get the shampoo off, she plunged back into the pool, making sure that she stayed under water long enough to get all the shampoo off.

When Diana emerged from the river, she reached for the towel that she had left on a large rock on the shore. She heard a sound to her left toward the bushes, and caught sight of a movement in her direction. She turned and looked straight at the face of a huge grizzly bear. The bear apparently enjoyed fishing in the pool. Screaming, she ran naked toward the cooking area.

Looking up, Jim shouted, "Stop! Kneel down on the ground and double up! Cover your head with your hands! Put your head between your legs if you can." Somehow, she made herself follow his instructions. Slowly, Jim walked toward her, but by then the bear was where she was kneeling. Diana and Jim were able to smell the foul, spoiled-fish breath of the bear. The bear then abruptly stood up on his hind legs and let out a tremendous roar, which Josh, David, and Tom heard.

"Don't move," Jim said. "Bears often charge like this, but will not attack if they do not feel threatened."

After what seemed like an eternity, the bear appeared to smell the chicken that was by then burning on the grill. The bear moved to the grill to pick up the meat. Not seeing the blue flame from the propane burners, his paw touched the grill. With a roar of pure agony, the bear went galloping off into the underbrush. Jim gently reached down and picked Diana up. Sobbing, she turned and clung to him. He could not suppress an erection. She felt the movement against her body, and hid her smile of pleasure against his shoulder.

"I had better get dressed."

He nodded in agreement. She took five or six steps, then turned halfway around, her body becoming silhouetted as she did so, and quietly said, "Thanks."

Once again, Jim just nodded, hoping that she had not noticed the bulge in his pants, which he could not stop when he saw her slender abdomen and perfectly straight breasts. As she walked away toward he tent, her buttocks made exceptionally sexy moves because she had to step over and around boulders in her bare feet. She looked back at him again as she entered her tent, and he waved.

After they heard the second roar of the grizzly, David, Josh, and Tom rushed back down the shallow stream as fast as they could, terrified about what they might find. However, when they finally reached camp, all was calm and peaceful. Diana had on fresh clothes, and Jim had rescued the remaining chicken breasts from burning up on the grill. Over a few beers, they related the story of the bear encounter, or at least most of the story. Tom perceived a certain embarrassment in both Jim and Diana. He had thought that they would still be emotionally shaken by the experience.

After dinner, David asked Josh, "Would you mind helping me move our tent and belongings away from the bushes, and closer to your two tents?"

"Sure," Josh said.

About two o'clock in the morning, Diana awakened with a dull headache and some vague nausea. Actually, given the clearness of the night, Tom had seen the aurora borealis and had awakened everyone in the camp at around midnight, so Diana had already been up earlier. She immediately took her migraine medicine, hoping to abort an attack. By dawn, though, she had a full-blown migraine and was unable to eat breakfast because of the nausea. Diana told Jim and David that she could paddle, but after an hour on the river it was obvious that she was of no help to David in the canoe. None of the medication that she had brought along for her migraines was working, and she was down to her last pill.

During a mid-morning break, Jim and Josh tested the emergency radio transmitter, in case they had to call the Royal Canadian Mounted Police for a helicopter evacuation for Diana. Disturbingly, they found that the batteries were dead. Jim embarrassingly proclaimed, "I checked the batteries before we left Anchorage, and they were fully charged. I don't know what happened to them."

At about the same time, the daily catamaran between Eagle and Dawson passed by on the other side of the river, but they had no way to call the vessel. Jim, Tom, and Josh knew this meant that if they had a genuine emergency, they were in trouble, but no one talked about it. Their pace downriver slowed to the speed of a raft because Diana was unable to help David paddle. At lunch, Tom suggested to Jim, "Let's split up the canoes. I can put her in the bow of our canoe, and Josh can take over the stern of the Wortham canoe."

Instead, Jim elected to put Diana in the bow of his canoe, and put more of the heavy items in the McClamrock canoe. "As the guide,

I can't let you do that, Tom, but I appreciate your offer," Jim said. "This is my responsibility. Josh, you take the stern position in the Wortham canoe, if that is okay with your dad. David, you get in the bow."

Tom moved into the bow seat facing toward the stern to have better control of his canoe since he would be paddling by himself. A bed of sorts was made for Diana in Jim's canoe, utilizing the tent bags and the dry bags containing everyone's clothes. She leaned backward toward the prow of the canoe, and draped her legs over the forward seat. Tom said to Diana, "You might want to wear your sunglasses and cover your eyes with a jacket or a towel to provide as much darkness as possible. Diana did as Tom suggested. The little convoy of canoes, so rearranged, struck out again on the mighty Yukon. Jim and Tom paddled silently in their respective canoes.

The only sounds came from the Wortham canoe, where Josh diplomatically and patiently tried to teach David some of the basic paddle strokes. Tom heard Josh say, "David, there is no need for you to learn anything complicated, such as the J-stroke, since that is a stroke done from the stern. You just need to learn to pull your stroke straight back from out front of the bow until the paddle is in the middle of the canoe."

"Okay."

"Also, try to avoid splashing me with water from your paddle," Josh said.

"Got it."

Tom thought to himself that he should have brought along narcotics for pain relief, in the event someone needed it. He had been given a prescription for Percocet by his dentist, who had camped out in Alaska with her husband on two occasions and was therefore aware of the vast wilderness. As a physician, he had known that he would be expected to have medicine available, and he had brought along appropriate medicine to treat bacterial diarrhea, giardiasis, and cystitis, but nothing for pain. He simply forgot to fill the prescription for Percocet. He was also disturbed that Diana had come on a wilderness trip unprepared to deal with her migraines, and had put the entire expedition in jeopardy.

Diana had taken her last remaining migraine pill, and as soon as the journey down the river resumed, she began to feel better. So she took the jacket off of her eyes. That gave her a chance to talk quietly and privately with Jim. She was in awe of his poise and courage during the episode with the bear. In addition, she was intrigued by his rugged good looks and his physique. Glancing over at David in the following canoe, she could not help being struck with the physical differences in the two men.

Because the weather had warmed up to about eighty-five degrees, Diana took off her sweater, leaving her upper body clothed only in a T-shirt, and she was not wearing a bra. Quietly, she said, "Jim, this reminds me of being in Venice, and you are my gondolier."

Never having been to Venice, Jim made no reply. For the remainder of the next few miles, she remained silent, but periodically sneaked a peek at Jim under her sunglasses, observing the muscles of his arms as he paddled the canoe unassisted down the river. Since he obviously had to look forward, he could not help but observe the splendid figure of the woman lying in front of him.

"Jim, do you work out regularly, or are you just naturally in good shape?"

"Just naturally, I guess."

Diana said, "Did you know that Ursula Andress used to say that she stayed in shape by having sex?"

"That's interesting," Jim replied.

Diana's fascination with Jim caused her to reflect back on her first love, Warren Musgrove, the incredibly handsome and well-built star quarterback in her high school class. She had become pregnant at sixteen, and they had gotten married when they were both seniors in high school. A year later, her parents had forced her to divorce him because he was, as they said, "Not from the right side of the tracks." Warren was so distraught over their separation that he joined the army and became a Green Beret.

During two tours in Vietnam, he was awarded the Silver Star, the Bronze Star for gallantry, and two Purple Hearts. Unfortunately, he accidentally was sprayed several times with Agent Orange, and he had been chronically ill ever since returning from Vietnam. Her affection for him had never died, and she felt terribly guilty about what had happened to him. She had seen him once since his return from Vietnam, but his wasted appearance caused her so much distress and guilt that she never made an effort to visit with him again.

At around four o'clock, Jim saw an island in the distance in the middle of the river with enough aspen trees to provide shade for Diana .He motioned with his paddle for the other canoes to head toward the island. The sandbar at the head of the island was remarkably free of boulders. Therefore, setting up the tents was very easy. Before dinner, Josh, Tom, and Jim had a few beers, while the Worthams went on a walk to the end of the sandbar, about a half-mile away.

Josh said to Jim, "Hey, we'd better get to Eagle pretty soon. We're getting low on beer."

"We'll be there soon enough, Josh," replied Jim.

"By the way, Jim, what's for dinner?" said Josh.

"Broccoli and cheese lasagna."

"No meat?"

"No, the Worthams are vegetarians, and I tried to accommodate their diet," Jim responded.

"Man, I could use some meat."

"I'm sorry," Jim said.

Tom sat quietly. *How did we get stuck with the Worthams?* he thought.

After they all finished their vegetable-pasta-cheese dinner, Tom shared his port with Josh and Jim. Twilight came earlier than usual that night, a sign that winter was coming soon. They all turned in earlier than the usual hour. At around ten o'clock that night, Diana awoke and was starving. Because of the nausea associated with the migraine, she had eaten very little all day. David was sound asleep and snoring softly. She very quietly unzipped the door of their tent, wearing only a T-shirt and jogging pants, and headed for the camp kitchen site, which was always placed at a respectable distance from the tents, except for Jim's, because of the bears.

As quietly as possible, she unsnapped the latches on the food containers, but one of the latches made a loud slapping sound as she opened it. Peering into the container by the dim light created by the stars and the aurora borealis, she could not find any food. Suddenly, she heard a voice behind softly say, "Can I help you?" Startled, she turned to see Jim standing behind her, clad only in jogging pants. She found herself staring at the taut muscles of his abdomen, a perfect so-called six-pack.

"I'm starving," she said, stammering from the surprise and excitement of seeing Jim with his shirt off. "I, I, I was hoping to find a granola bar or something."

"I have some in my tent," he said. "Come with me."

She followed him obediently into his tent. He fumbled in his day pack until he found a granola bar, and cleared his gear from the side of the tent so that she could crawl inside and find a place to sit.

"Oatmeal raisin okay?" he asked her.

"Sure."

He watched her slowly put the bar into her mouth, moving it back and forth two or three times before gently biting down on it. Lying on his sleeping bag, he leaned on his elbow as he watched her mouth. When she was finished, she passed her tongue over her lips one or two times, as she observed his facial expression. Without saying a word, she removed her T-shirt, revealing her bare breasts and her flat abdomen in the dim light. Just as quickly, she pushed him down onto his sleeping bag.

"We shouldn't be doing this," he said.

"I know," she replied as she pulled down his pants, and then swiftly removed her pants. She lay down on top of him, and almost immediately his penis was in her vagina. Jim had not had sex for two months because of his wife's pregnancy. He knew that that was not an excuse or a justification for having sex with this woman. And, yet, he could not resist her advances. Initially, he tried to resist the lunges of her body against his, but soon he succumbed.

After a rest of ten or fifteen minutes, she began to caress him. Amazed, he found himself aroused again. He took charge, fondling her breasts and her pubic area until she was begging him for relief, whispering over and over again, "Hurry, hurry, hurry!" Slowly, he obliged her, using painfully slow thrusts of his penis into the deepest recesses of her vagina, until she was moaning in ecstasy. Finally, they both collapsed. After an hour or so, she sneaked back into her tent, apparently never awakening David. At dawn, she slipped out of the tent to the nearby woods to urinate, and to cleanse herself with Baby Wipes.

As the sun came up over the horizon, they all stumbled out of their tents and began the process of breaking camp. After a hearty breakfast of pancakes and sausage, they were on their way again. Tom could not eat the sausage because it reminded him of the frostbitten toe, which he had kissed a few nights earlier in Dawson at the SoughDough Saloon.

"Josh, look at all of the contrails," Tom exclaimed. "Where do you think those planes are flying from? Anchorage to Europe, or are they military jets out of Elmendorf Air Base?"

"I think those planes are probably taking the Great Circle Route from Tokyo and Hong Kong to Europe," Josh said. "It must be very cold up there to be making the contrails, and look at how the wind is changing their shape."

Back in their canoes, Diana with David and Josh with Tom, they approached a high cliff, where a fish trap came into view just a hundred yards or so ahead. Jim turned his canoe to the right again and said, "Migrating salmon are caught between the paddles of the rotating wheel in the fish trap. The downward current turns the paddles, like a Ferris wheel at a carnival, thus causing the trap to rotate on its axis. The fish that enter the trap as they go upriver cannot escape because of the rotation of the wheel. These fish are then dried, and are critical for the survival of the residents who live near the Yukon River all year. These year-round residents are allowed to catch and kill whatever they need, with no limits and no seasonal restrictions, as long as they catch and kill only what they truly need for survival. This is known as the subsistence law."

At about the same time, Jim yelled out, "There's a moose on the other bank." And, sure enough, there was a cow moose drinking water on the edge of the river.

Josh said, "Where's her calf?"

"Don't know. Maybe he is in the bushes behind her. We certainly don't want to go over there to check it out," Jim said.

Diana and David said nothing, which Tom assumed to be their lack of interest, or, he thought, *Perhaps they are just cooler than Josh and me.*

A few miles farther downstream, there was a sudden and violent burst of wind on their starboard side. The temperature dropped at least twenty degrees over the next ten to fifteen minutes. When they turned a bend in the river, so that they were now facing due north, whitecaps began to splash over the bows of the canoes. The strong north wind blowing against the strong river current was creating the appearance of the surf in the Gulf of Mexico.

Tom shouted to Jim, "We'd better get out of this before we have a catastrophe."

"Okay, follow me," Jim yelled.

Jim was again paddling by himself in the lead, with David and Diana behind him, followed by the McClamrocks. They all headed for a rocky sandbar on the eastern side of the river where there was some protection from the wind. By that time, Tom and Josh estimated the wind velocity to be thirty-five knots. Sand on a bar on the western side of the river was blowing like a sandstorm in the desert, in spite of the fact that it was moist.

"Damn it, David! Get control of your canoe!" Tom yelled.

"I'm trying, you asshole," David yelled back.

Just as they had almost reached the sandbar, a sudden gust caught the Wortham canoe, blowing it directly into the path of the McClamrock canoe and causing the McClamrock canoe to strike the Wortham canoe amidships. This knocked the canoe on its side, dumping Diana, David, and all of the contents of the canoe into the river. Since they were so close to each other, the McClamrocks were able to reach the Worthams immediately. Tom and Josh obviously could not haul them into their canoe without risking another capsizing.

Josh yelled, "Hold onto the middle part of the gunwales."

"Don't get on the same side. David," Tom said. "You get on the right side, and Diana, you hang onto the left side." *Why am I trying to save the life of this guy who just called me an asshole?* Tom thought. They paddled as fast as they could with the two human sea anchors slowing them down and making it difficult for Tom and Josh to pull a full paddle stroke. The two people hanging on the sides of the canoe made it almost impossible to paddle in the high waves and winds.

Tom said, "Josh, I guess that you know full well that we have about five minutes before hypothermia begins to set in."

"Yep."

Tom knew that if they did not get the Worthams warm and dry in a very few minutes, the mental deterioration associated with hypothermia would show itself, and they might not then be able to get them to cooperate with efforts to save them. Tom and Josh reached the shore just in time, before David and Diana began to lose their grip on the gunwales. In the meantime, Jim had been able to turn around, paddle upriver against the current, and retrieve the dry bags containing the Worthams' clothes and sleeping bags, but the other items and their canoe were gone.

By the time Jim arrived on the shore with the dry bags, Tom and Josh had managed to get Diana and David out of their wet clothes. They lent the Worthams some of their own clothes, along with their jackets. They then opened the Worthams' dry bags, and ordered them to get into their sleeping bags. David and Diana were shivering uncontrollably, but Tom was pleased that they were still intact mentally. He knew that shivering was a good sign, now that they were in dry warm clothes, and that the shivering would cease as soon as their core body temperature returned to normal.

With the wind blowing as it was, starting a fire on an open beach was impossible. Jim and Tom and Josh stood silently beside each other, slightly distant from the Worthams. They knew they had a real problem. Tom thought, *Here we are stuck on a sandbar covered with too many large boulders to comfortably lie down, with the wind blowing at thirty-five knots, with gusts up to fifty. In addition, we only have two canoes for five people, and two of the people have just barely escaped hypothermia. Shit!*

"What's that, Dad?"

Tom was startled. *Had I been mumbling to myself?* "Just thinking out loud," Tom replied, trying desperately to avoid showing any sign of panic to Josh.

After sitting and trying to lie on the rocks, all the while hoping that the wind would die down, Tom said, "Josh, I can't lie here on these rocks any longer. Let's go see if we can find a sandy part of this beach."

Leaving Jim to watch Diana and David in their sleeping bags, Tom and Josh went about fifty or sixty yards down the river. Jim yelled out, "Wait! It's not going to get any better on this spit of land. We've got to move on downstream. Let's get back in the canoes, and stay close to shore in case we have another capsizing."

So they started out again. Jim, Diane, and David were in the front canoe, and Josh and Tom were in the rear. About one hundred yards downriver from where they had launched their canoes, Jim spotted a beautiful sandy stretch of beach, just about fifty yards from where Josh and Tom had been standing when he called to them to turn back. He abruptly pulled into shore, and Tom and Josh followed. By this time, the gusts of wind were at least fifty knots, by all of their estimates. With considerable difficulty, they pitched their tents. Jim moved into the McClamrock tent, and let Diane and David have his, since theirs had been lost. The wind was blowing so hard that they had to put fifteen or sixteen boulders about the size of coconuts around the edges of the tent floor to keep the tent from blowing away. In addition, they put stakes into the tent holders, with boulders on top of the stakes.

After the tents were secure, Jim said, "It must be obvious to everyone that starting a fire, even a propane one, is impossible in this wind. So I brought along some sardines, Vienna sausage, cheese, and crackers for just such an emergency. I know that you, David and Diana, are vegetarians, but I would urge you to eat some of this food, so that you will have some strength."

"I'll just eat cheese and crackers," David said.

"I might try a sardine," said Diana. "I've heard that they are good for your heart."

"That's true," Tom said.

They all turned in early that evening, even before darkness had descended. The wind blew so fiercely that night that their tents shook enough to awaken them. Tom was glad that there were three of them in their tent to weigh it down. In spite of their weight, at times they thought that the tent might blow away like a tumbleweed, and be carried right into the river with the three of them inside.

Sometime during one of these awakenings, Tom looked out and saw an amazing display of the Northern Lights. He woke everyone, since he felt certain that they all would not want to miss the spectacle. Jim had seen it many times in the past, so he stayed in the tent. Josh crawled out just enough for his head to be sticking out of the tent, and then he quickly slid back inside, like a tortoise. Tom could not tell whether David and Diana acknowledged his untimely wake-up call. Because there were no clouds in the cold sky, the stars were incredibly bright, giving the appearance of being right on top of them, like in a planetarium. The Milky Way was directly above them, and to the north there was a broad wavy band of a mixture of green, yellow, and red lights moving like a drapery blowing in the wind. Tom knew it must be the aurora borealis.

Tom thought of the psalmist's words: "When I look at your heavens, the work of your fingers, the moon and the stars that you have established, what are human beings that you are mindful of them, mortals that you care for them?" At around two o'clock in the morning, the thermometer on Tom's watch read twenty-one degrees Fahrenheit. Combined with a thirty-five to fifty knot wind that probably equated to a windchill factor of roughly twelve to fifteen degrees. He could not believe the temperature had dropped sixty degrees within a twelve-hour period. He said to himself, "I guess that this is what it means to be in the Arctic."

By dawn, they were all exhausted. However, shortly after dawn, the wind died. Jim hurriedly got them moving because he suspected that they had a brief window of opportunity to paddle before another blast of cold wind arrived. Jim wanted them to reach their next campsite at the ghost town of Fortymile.

Jim said, "Before we get into our canoes, let me tell you a little bit about our next destination." Jim was trying to speak as if nothing bad had happened the previous day, as if this was just another normal day on the river.

"In 1886, two prospectors found gold on the Fortymile River, a tributary of the Yukon. When word got out, there was an avalanche of miners who mined the Fortymile extensively. The miners' supply base at the mouth of the Fortymile River became the town of Fortymile. At one time, Fortymile had a population of one thousand people, served by six saloons, several restaurants, a number of doctors and blacksmiths, a watchmaker, a dressmaker, a library, a theatre, and the Yukon Territory's first post office. Today, the town is deserted, but many buildings are still standing and are in a terrible state of repair. The Canadian government has declared the site a national historic location, and has provided an outdoor toilet and a simple fireplace with a grill."

"A real toilet?" asked Diana.

"Well, sort of, but with no running water or mirrors with lights," quipped Jim.

"I like the idea of a grill," piped up Josh.

They reached Fortymile around three o'clock in the afternoon, just as the wind picked up again. To beach the canoes, they had two choices: They could paddle up the swiftly flowing Fortymile River, or land on a large mudflat on the upriver side of the junction of the Fortymile with the Yukon. Jim reasoned that it would be wiser to land on the mudflat. If anyone was unable to handle the current in the Fortymile, there was no way to backtrack up the Yukon to the mudflat because of the strong current in the Yukon. As it turned out, he made the wrong choice.

When they stepped out of their canoes, they immediately began to sink into the mud. Jim ordered all of them to get off the mudflat up onto dry land, and he said that he would take care of the canoes. Tom ignored him, and struggled to drag his canoe through the shallow water on the edge of the mudflat, until he could reach an area of solid ground. The work was exhausting because the canoe was not afloat, and because walking through the mud was extremely difficult.

Jim yelled to Tom, "Whatever you do, don't stop, or you'll get stuck!"

As long as Tom kept moving, he was all right. However, once he stopped for a few seconds to rest, and he was immediately up to his knees in mud and could not extract himself. Seeing Tom's predicament, Jim rushed over to help, and literally picked him up out of the mud. Tom lost a boot in the process, but, fortunately, he was able to pull it out of the mud. After what seemed like an eternity, they were able to actually walk on their knees and shins on the mud, and then were able to pull the canoes up on a solid bank of the Fortymile River. As they began to unload the canoes, Tom told himself, "I don't think that I will need a treadmill EKG at my next checkup."

Meanwhile, Josh, David, and Diana had gone on up the embankment to check out the campsite, oblivious to the plight of Tom and Jim. The campsite was on a grassy plateau of sorts, about fifty feet above the Fortymile and one hundred yards from where it joined the Yukon. This provided them with a magnificent view of both rivers. Diana had already discovered the outdoor toilet, which had been built by the Canadian Park Service. They pitched their tents in a soft grassy field near two of the old deserted buildings. The setting reminded Josh and Tom somewhat of the fishing camp on the Kenai River, where they had spent three days and nights prior to joining the Yukon wilderness trip.

"Hey, Josh, that cabin there on the Kenai Peninsula, with real beds, showers, toilets, and a lodge with tables and chairs and real napkins, looks very luxurious now, doesn't it?"

"Yes, but this is still better than sleeping on a sandbar," Josh replied.

Although the park service had built a fireplace with a grill, they had lost all of the meat in the capsized canoe. Josh remembered that they had passed a small fish wheel trap about a mile up the Yukon on the Fortymile side of the river. "Let's go see if we can get some fish out of the trap. I need some meat to eat," he said.

Jim, Josh, and Tom struck out for the fish wheel. The walking was easy because of the grass, and they reached the site of the fish wheel quickly.

"Now what do we do?" Tom asked.

It was obvious that Jim had never been this close to a fish wheel. He began to study it intensely, watching the rhythmical movement of the blade as the current turned the wheel over and over. Because of the murky water they could not tell if there were any fish in the trap. They finally decided to stick a large branch into the bottom of the river, and then let the blade slam into it, holding it in place while Jim crawled into the trap to try to retrieve some salmon.

Jim took off all of his clothes, and cautiously climbed into the trap. After running his hands around the trap for a few seconds, he grabbed a large eight- or ten-pound whitefish, and began to climb out of the trap. As he reached the bank and handed the fish to Josh, his right foot accidentally kicked the limb, knocking it loose from the bottom of the river. The paddle slammed down on his left leg, about halfway between the ankle and the knee. The leg bent double, and was on the verge of being crudely amputated, when Josh dashed over, grabbed the paddle, and somehow through superhuman strength was able to pull the paddle up high enough for Tom to pull Jim's leg out of the trap.

Jim was moaning in agony, and blood was pouring out of the open fracture on his left leg. Both the tibia and the fibula had been broken. Both bones were protruding. Fortunately, Jim did not have on his pants, thus providing Tom with a good view of the fracture site. Tom quickly took the belt from Jim's pants and made a tourniquet, which he applied above Jim's knee.

"Josh, find some one-inch branches from some of those birch trees, and then help me make a splint using our belts to secure the branches." They gently picked Jim up, locking their arms under his buttocks, and stumbled back to camp. Jim heroically held the fish in his lap.

"Jim, I need for you to remind me to periodically loosen that belt on your leg, so you get some blood to your lower leg," Tom said.

"Okay, Doc, I'll try to remember."

Never having been interested in orthopedics in medical school, Tom consequently knew very little about bone fractures, other than what he had learned as a Boy Scout. Fearing that something like Jim's accident might happen, he had brought a paperback copy of the *Field Guide to Wilderness Medicine*. As soon as they laid Jim down at camp, he found the book. Based on what he could glean from the section on leg fractures, he tried to figure out how he could fashion a splint better than one made out of tree branches. In the meantime, he released the tension on the hastily rigged tourniquet. Fortunately, the bleeding did not resume.

"Diana and David, please try to find the first aid kit in Jim's dry bags," Tom said. Looking around, he saw several decrepit old buildings with plenty of wooden planks that could be used to make a better splint. First, he cleaned the open wound with some Baby Wipes, and then applied a gauze pad from the first aid kit. He did not consider manipulating the protruding bone fragments. After wrapping the gauze pad over the gaping wound, he placed Jim's life vest over the lower leg.

"Okay, Josh, I need you to help me break two thin planks from one of those old buildings."

In less than five minutes, Josh returned with the boards.

"Okay, now we need to place a short board across the foot of the two longer boards, like you see in this drawing in the book."

"Why not use the throw rope from Jim's canoe to tie his ankle to the short footboard, and use the remainder of the rope to secure the long boards to his leg?" Josh suggested.

"Excellent idea," Tom said.

Jim's life vest provided a very adequate cushion between the boards and the broken leg. There were no pain medications in the first aid kit, so periodically Tom gave Jim sips of the port and the Canadian whisky he had brought along. After completing the first aid on the leg as best they could, Josh and Tom turned to preparing dinner. They knew that they all needed nourishment, especially Jim. The air temperature was falling again, and it was apparent that another cold night was approaching. Josh got the fire started while Tom gutted the fish, and cut the fish into two large filets, leaving the scales on. And then Tom made a sauce of oranges, butter, and Worcestershire sauce, with which Josh basted the filets as he cooked them over the fire. Even Jim ate heartily, in spite of his pain.

Tom thought back on the accident, and what he and Josh had heard as they had approached the camp at Forty Mile while carrying Jim back from the fish trap. They could hear Diana and David yelling at each other. When they had gotten closer, they heard David say, "Have you been sleeping with Jim?"

"What's it to you?"

With that, Tom and Josh heard a loud slap. "You bastard! I'm going to leave you," Diana yelled.

At about that time, Tom and Josh arrived on the scene with Jim, and Diana and David both came rushing over to see what had happened. One side of Diana's face was bright red in lines. It was apparent who had sustained the loud slap that they had heard as they neared the campsite.

When darkness fell that night, the temperature dropped precipitously. The wind had died, which eliminated the windchill factor. Diana apparently refused to sleep in the tent with David, but since there were three people in the only other tent, she had no choice but to sleep outside. This made Tom, Jim, and Josh very uncomfortable, but there was nothing they could do about it, since it was a personal matter between Diana and David. Fortunately, all of the sleeping bags had hoods, which meant that her head would be protected. Also, there were no cloud formations to suggest impending rain or snow that night. However, the lack of clouds made the temperature plunge even more because there was nothing to trap the day's heat and keep it close to the surface of the earth.

Even though the nights were becoming longer with the rapidly approaching winter, dawn still occurred between 4:30 and 5:00 AM. At around 6:30 AM, Tom crawled out of his sleeping bag to try to put some sort of breakfast together, since Jim was obviously out of commission. He also wanted them to get Jim downriver to Eagle as soon as possible to air evacuate him to a hospital. After finding some muffins and yogurt and making cold coffee with chocolate, he awakened Josh and Jim, and brought Jim some breakfast. He then awakened David. To Tom's amazement, Diana was not in the tent.

"Where is Diana, David?"

"I don't know," David replied. "She wanted to sleep outside on our last night out on the river."

"Well, I don't see her here in camp. Don't you think we had better try to find her?"

"Sure, of course."

"Josh, come help us look for Diana," Tom said.

They searched the grassy plateau of the campsite to no avail. Finally, Josh went to the cliff overlooking the two rivers. To his dismay, there was only one canoe. Apparently, in the early dawn light, she had taken her sleeping bag and her personal dry bag, and shoved off down the Fortymile River by herself, leaving the four of them with one canoe, and Jim with a compound fracture of the lower leg.

"Damn, damn, damn it!" Tom snorted. "Is your wife nuts, or something?"

47

"Yes, in fact she suffers from manic depression," David replied quietly. "She didn't bring her lithium on this trip because she decided that she didn't need it anymore."

"How stupid could she be? Doesn't she know that she has to take lithium forever to keep her condition under control?" Tom asked.

"Yes, she knows that, but periodically she thinks that she can get off of it."

"Well, she's left us in a hell of a mess. In addition, she doesn't seem to know anything about canoeing. She's probably sitting in the stern seat, trying to paddle a tandem canoe. She'll have a hell of a time controlling it, if she doesn't figure out that she needs to sit in the bow seat turned around."

Meekly, David said, "I hope she doesn't capsize again."

"Shit!" snorted Tom again. "To hell with her! What about the mess she's left us in? We have one canoe for four men, and one of 'em has a broken leg."

Realizing that he had to get control of himself, or else he could create panic, Tom walked away from David and Josh for a few minutes, mumbling to himself, "What a fucking mess this woman has gotten us into!"

After Tom composed himself, he returned to where Josh and David were standing and said, "Okay, let's get organized. We need to have a conference. Let's all go talk this over with Jim."

Jim had been left in the tent while the search for Diana was taking place, since there was nothing that he could do to help. When they aroused Jim, who had fallen asleep again, Tom found him to be in somewhat of a daze, which Tom assumed was probably due to the pain. Nevertheless, Tom thought that, in fairness to the others, he should seek Jim's opinion and advice.

After explaining the situation to Jim, without eliciting any coherent response, Tom said, "Okay, this is what we have to do. Josh, you and David take Jim to Eagle in the canoe, and I'll walk up the Fortymile River to the bridge on the Taylor Highway. When you get to Eagle, go to the ranger station and get them to arrange for an air evacuation for Jim. After that is done, pay someone to come up the Taylor Highway to pick me up. Here's all of my money. It should be around a thousand dollars in cash, plus here are some travelers checks. Okay?"

"No. I can't leave you here."

"Josh, we don't have a choice. You could see that Jim didn't have any other ideas." Winking, Tom said, "Look, your mother would kill me if I came home without you. So I'll take my chances here. You and I are the strongest people. David is not equipped to survive out here. So one of us has to stay, and one of us has to get Jim to a hospital. Jim will die if you don't get him to Eagle."

Tom gestured toward the remaining canoe and said, "Now, David you get in the bow of the canoe—that's the front, and Josh will take the stern. David, remember to dig the paddle into the water, and then pull backward with vigor. Josh is going to need your help. Be careful to not pull too vigorously, so that you turn the canoe over. We need to put all of the dry bags with clothes in the bottom of the canoe, and make a bed for Jim, like a couch, with his head up and facing forward, so that he can help navigate. Okay, let's get going. I need to get one change of clothes out of my dry bag before you load it, plus my gloves and my sleeping bag."

An hour later, the canoe was loaded with enough food and water for the three men, with Jim propped up on the dry bags and sleeping bags in the middle of the canoe. Tom handed Josh his copy of the *Yukon River Guide*, and hugged him. Neither of them could speak. As Josh reached the prow of the canoe, he suddenly turned around and came back to give Tom another hug. Tears were in his eyes as he got into the canoe. Tom pushed them off, and stood on the bank as they headed out into the Fortymile. When they reached the junction with the Yukon, Josh waved his paddle in the air from side to side, without turning around, and then they were gone. The loneliness was sickening for Tom. The last time he had felt like this was when he boarded a flight to Vietnam thirty-seven years earlier. He made himself shake it off, and get himself ready for his upcoming trek.

Diana had made remarkably good time since departing the campsite at Fortymile. Judging from her copy of the *Yukon River Guide*, she had successfully passed several islands and the twin eddies, a particularly tricky part of the river. Rounding a bend, she saw two mesas, one on each side of the river. Her guidebook said that these were the Old Man and Old Woman Rocks. According to Han legend, these rocks were once one rock in the middle of the river. They lived together as husband and wife, but separated over a marital dispute. Old Woman Rock was angry and pushed Old Man Rock across the river. She then drifted north, while he drifted south. *How fitting for my situation*, Diana thought.

In spite of the fact that she was sitting in the stern instead of in the bow, sitting backwards, she found that canoeing down the river by herself had been remarkably easy and uneventful. Of course, she recognized that the canoe had no weight other than that of her body, and that the river current was quite strong. She did regret not having brought some water along, as well as some food other than a few bags of potato chips and pretzels. She hated to think about drinking that dirty-looking river water, but she knew that it was probably inevitable. Just about that time, she heard the sound of a waterfall, and realized that a beautiful little stream was entering the river on the right side of the river. She frantically paddled the canoe toward the stream, and proudly was able to beach the canoe just below the stream entrance. She then disembarked from the canoe, and walked up to the pristine little tributary. Kneeling down, she scooped large handfuls of clear water into her mouth.

After a brief rest and toilet break, Diana climbed back into the canoe, this time sitting in the bow, since it was the most accessible part of the canoe, not realizing that she had actually done herself a favor. She was amazed at how much easier she found the canoe to steer, and began to actually enjoy the experience. She threaded her way through the dozen islands with the deftness of an experienced river guide. Glancing at her guidebook, she noted with pleasure that she was not very many miles from the Canadian and United States border.

She began to wonder if and when the others, especially David and Jim, had noticed that she was gone. She also wondered if they were at that moment trying to catch up with her. *Oh, hell!* she thought. *I left them with only one canoe. I forgot that we had lost one canoe when David and I turned over in the windstorm. Oh, my God, what have I done? And, Jim has a broken leg.* She covered her face in her hands and wept.

When she had first entered the Yukon River from the Fortymile, the dawn sky had been brilliantly clear. The temperature at that time was in the low thirties. Now, heavy looking gray clouds were accumulating, and the temperature was dropping. She assumed that it was getting colder because the clouds were obscuring the sun. Fortunately, the wind was not blowing like it had a few days earlier.

Diana contemplated stopping to camp and rest. However, the thought of being on a lonely beach by herself, with the threat of bears, wolves, and moose, made her decide to push on toward Eagle and escape back to civilization. At twilight, she saw two small flags on the left side of the river, one red and white, with a red maple leaf in the center, and the familiar Stars and Stripes. She knew from her guidebook that she was at the Canadian and United States border, and only twelve to fifteen miles from Eagle. Even though it was beginning to get dark, she continued on downriver.

Looking ahead, which was due north at that point in the river, she saw what looked to be a cloud bank or fog. As she got closer, she realized that it also was moving toward her. To her amazement, she realized that it was snow. Shivering, she grabbed her ski coat, and got it on as quickly as she could. Now she could not see anything. Neither bank was visible. She decided that probably the wisest thing to do would be to just drift. She pulled the hood of her ski jacket over her head, slid down into the bottom of the canoe, and leaned back against the seat. Her life jacket made a relatively comfortable cushion to lean against. She was soon sound asleep.

After Josh, Jim, and David had rounded a bend in the Yukon, Tom scurried around the campsite to get ready to leave. Josh and David had helped him pack the tents in the tent bags. Tom put a note in each bag, giving the name of the Alaska-Yukon Wilderness Tours, and then put the tent bags in one of the old buildings that still had a roof. Feeling a chill, he looked up, and realized that dark gray clouds were accumulating. *Could these be snow clouds?* he wondered.

This thought caused him to redouble his efforts to get moving toward the bridge over the river. He hurriedly packed all of the remaining granola bars and potato chips, and put them in Ziploc bags. He decided that water was too heavy to carry, and that he would have to drink river water and worry about giardiasis later. After all, he had brought along Flagyl anyhow; so, he could always treat himself for giardiasis, an illness brought on by parasitic organism sometimes found in rivers and streams. He did bring a small amount of coffee and hot chocolate mix.

With the food and some emergency flares, plus one change of pants, shirt, and long underwear, there was not room in the day pack for his sleeping bag. Fortunately, the expandable cords on the back of the pack allowed room for the sleeping bag. With a final scan of the campsite, and a wistful glance down the Yukon, he struck out, heading up the Fortymile River. The time was approximately ten o'clock in the morning. As he left the campsite, light snow was beginning to fall. He was glad that he had not forgotten his broad-brim waterproof hat. Tom had left his gloves in Anchorage, but Jim had given him his extra pair.

Initially, he walked along the edge of the river, even though the rocks made it difficult to keep his balance. Eventually, he came to a point where a high cliff came straight into the river. To have kept going on that track would have meant that he had to walk in the river. As cold as it was now, he thought it unwise to get wet. Instead, he climbed up a steep embankment to reach a ridge high above the river. To move upriver, he struggled through thick underbrush, being careful to not get so close to the cliff's edge that he might fall off into the river. Tom wished that he had a machete, so that he could have cut through the underbrush instead of having to fight it every step he took.

At one point, he went back down to the river's edge, partly to get some water to drink. By this time the snow was coming down heavily, making visibility very poor. The rocks along the river's edge were slippery because of the snow. He reluctantly climbed back up to the high ground above the river, and, once again, struggled through the underbrush. He walked and climbed uphill for eight hours or so, until he saw a clearing ahead. He decided that he should stop and rest, and make himself eat something.

Ever since Josh had left, he had felt such loneliness that he felt no hunger, but he knew that he needed some calories. He ate a small bag of potato chips, which made him thirsty again, but he was not about to go back down to the river for a drink of water, and then have to climb back up the hill. So he caught a small collection of snow and put it in his mouth, somewhat lessening his thirst.

Alarmingly, it was beginning to get darker. Tom dreaded the thought of spending the night out in the woods alone in the cold and snow. He picked up the pace, reminding himself that if he fell and hurt his legs, he would be in deep trouble out there all by himself. Just as darkness was beginning to really set in, he saw the bridge in the distance through the falling snow. He figured that he must have climbed one thousand to fifteen hundred feet since he had left the camp at the junction of the Fortymile River and the Yukon.

He rushed ahead, and found a smooth level place under the bridge to put his sleeping bag. After leaving his gear, he quickly found some firewood lodged under the bridge. The wood was still dry because it had been protected from the snow. Fortunately, he had not forgotten matches in his haste to leave the camp. When the fire lit, he smiled to himself with a great sense of relief. At least he had the warm company of a fire, even if he did not have companions. Theoretically, this would also keep away wandering wild animals that were looking for food. The question was how to keep the fire going all night, and still get some much-needed sleep.

Josh and his group had moved downriver at a very fast pace. David had been trying hard to help with the paddling. He had even asked for constructive criticism from Jim and Josh to try to improve his paddling strokes. Jim helped Josh navigate through the islands and different channels, in spite of his pain. His lower leg was becoming numb. David had wanted to talk about Diana, and Josh and Jim let him talk freely. He was very chagrined over what she had done, and the danger that she had created for everyone.

According to David, as long as Diana faithfully took her lithium carbonate, her personality was very stable. However, when she stopped taking her medication, she exhibited wild mood swings. When depressed, she would not leave the bedroom, and David would have to bring her food and beverages. When in a manic phase, she would leave the house and hang out in bars, where she would pick up total strangers for one- night stands of sex. It was obvious that David had wanted Jim to hear about the one-night stand behavior.

After a few hours on the river, they stopped at an island to rest, and to take a toilet break. They gave Jim a coffee cup to use as a urinal to avoid moving him out of the canoe. While they were beached on the island, they noticed that the temperature had dropped significantly, and that the sky was covered with dark clouds. They decided that they probably should take the opportunity to put Jim in his sleeping bag. They unzipped the bag, slid one side under him, and then zipped the bag up. Just as they finished, light snow began to fall.

They pushed on until it was almost dark, never seeing Diana or her canoe, with almost no conversation among them. Josh had hoped that they might reach Eagle, but the worsening snowfall had interfered with their vision, and caused them to take the wrong channels from time to time.

Finally, Jim said, "Josh, I think it would be wise to stop for the night."

"I agree," said David. "I'm exhausted."

They beached the canoe on one of the islands in the Dozen Islands group, in a major bend of the river. Josh and David pulled the canoe well up onto the island, with Jim in it. Josh asked David, "Don't you think that we should just leave Jim in the canoe, rather than trying to move him?"

"I agree," David said. "What do you think, Jim?"

"Yes," Jim said, I think that would be smart."

After they each had a snack for supper, David and Josh placed their sleeping bags on the sand near the canoe, covered their heads with the hoods of their sleeping bags, and fell sound asleep.

Sometime during the night, Diana's canoe drifted into one of the alternate channels, where the water was only a few inches deep. The canoe came gently to a stop, not disturbing Diana's sleep. When the light returned at around five o'clock, she awakened and realized that the canoe was aground. The canoe also had three to four inches of snow in it, and she was covered in snow. Fortunately, her jacket was waterproof. However, she had failed to get into her sleeping bag, and was now very cold.

At first, she did not know which way she should take the canoe. She felt a wave of panic, being all alone with no one to consult or to guide her. Fleetingly, she thought about how nice it would be to have David and Jim near her, but then her survival instincts took over. She pulled herself together and shook off any feelings of remorse. Finally, through the dim dawn light, she could see that the main river channel lay behind her, and upriver about fifty yards. This meant that she would have to get out of the canoe, and drag it back upstream. When she stepped overboard, the water was very shallow at first. She then stepped off into some deeper water, where the water went over the top of her knee boot, soaking her feet and lower legs. Shivering, she got back into the canoe, almost flipping it over. She paddled fiercely, until she was clear of the gravel bar, and headed downstream again.

The snow continued to come down hard, blocking all vision beyond fifteen to twenty yards. Diana continued to paddle downstream with the current, but she did so very cautiously. There were only two islands in this stretch of the river, and she glided by them without ever seeing them. She was beginning to shiver much of the time, and she was having some difficulty concentrating on what she was doing. She repeatedly told herself, "Think, think, think! Pay attention, watch for the bank of the river, and look for the main channel." However, the shivering began to occupy all of her thoughts, and all she could think about was a warm bath.

The river began a sharp turn to the right, and she could feel the current moving in that direction. She found herself in a relatively narrow channel between two islands, and surmised that she was probably not in the main channel. She ran aground twice, but was able to pry the canoe forward without having to get out of the canoe into the water. If she had looked up and to the left, she might have seen the famous Eagle Bluff through the snow.

As she continued on down the river, she began to wonder why she had not reached Eagle, not realizing that she had passed it. She began to cry uncontrollably and did not know what to do. She began to think that she was on the Hudson River, near where her son lived. She then began to see visions of her first love, Warren, along with her baby son. Amazingly, she took off her clothes, the paradoxical phenomenon so typical of advanced stages of hypothermia.

Diana began to hallucinate that she was making love to Warren. Laying down in the bottom of the canoe, she became very sleepy. She no longer felt cold, only a bliss and peace that she had never felt in her life. She began to smile, and her breathing became more and more shallow. The canoe continued to drift north toward the Arctic Circle, like an ancient funeral barge. In the spring when the river had thawed, some Inuit fisherman found a canoe near the mouth of the Yukon River, and the well-preserved body of a naked woman.

At first light, Jim awakened Josh and David. He said, "Hey, guys, I think we should get going again." He had slept very little during the night. With the pain in his leg, plus the creeping numbness, he was very concerned that he might have lost the blood circulation to his leg. Sensing his concern, David and Josh got under way at sunrise. That was fortunate, since the snow soon began to fall heavier than ever. There was no way for them to see more than twenty to thirty yards ahead of them. Jim wisely advised them to stay close to the shore on the left side of the river, so that they could see the shoreline. He did not want them to miss the landing at Eagle.

After fifteen miles of paddling, Jim said, "Okay, guys, I see the landing. Josh steer the canoe onto the bank of the river."

David jumped out, and dragged the bow up onto the shore. When the canoe swung around, Josh climbed out of the stern, and then secured the bow line to a post.

"David, you stay with Jim, and I'll go get help," Josh said. He walked the half-mile to the village. No one in their right mind would be outside in the whirling snow and cold, and there was no one visible. He determined that he should head straight for the ranger station, as his father had advised him to do. As he passed by the Amundsen cabin on the road to the ranger station, he was amazed and thrilled to see a light through the window. Knocking on the door, Rusty Shaw opened the door. "Mr. Shaw, I'm Josh McClamrock. Do you remember my dad and me?"

"Of course, I do. Where is everybody else? What delayed you?"

"It's a long story. Right now, I need your help. Jim's in the canoe at the landing with a broken leg. David Wortham and I brought him down the river. We lost one canoe in a windstorm, and Diana Wortham ran off with another canoe."

"What?"

"Yeah, that's right. I'll have to tell you all about it later. Right now my dad says that we must get Jim to a hospital as soon as possible."

"By the way, where is your dad?"

"He's walking back up the Fortymile River to the bridge on the highway," Josh said.

"You've got to be kidding."

"Nope, I'm not. There was nothing else for us to do. There were four of us, with one canoe, and Jim had to lie down in the canoe because of the fracture."

"Oh, my God," Rusty said.

As Rusty and Josh approached the canoe, Jim thought that he was seeing a ghost. "Rusty, what in the world are you doing here?" Jim asked.

"When you didn't check in on time, I figured that something must be wrong. So I flew up here to check on you."

"Thank God you are here."

Josh, David, and Rusty gently picked Jim up out of the canoe, carried him in stages back to the Amundsen cabin, and put him in the single bed that Rusty had been using. After making everyone some coffee with hot chocolate, Rusty went back to the landing to secure the canoe high up on the bank of the river. While tending to that chore, he had time to contemplate how he was going to get Jim out of Eagle to a hospital. He knew that the weather forecast called for worsening snow conditions over the next three to four days. Blizzard conditions were predicted.

When Rusty got back to the cabin, he had made his decision. "Jim, I think that I need to fly you out of here before this snow gets worse. We can take out the front right seat of my plane, so you can stretch out your leg and sit on the backseat."

Josh said, "But how are you going to take off in this snow with essentially zero visibility?"

Rusty said, "We have at least a dozen emergency flares in the storage shed for these trips on the river. I'll get you and David to place them along both sides of the runway over by Fort Egbert. If I can see them through the snow, I should be able to build up enough airspeed to lift off. First, we'll have to de-ice the wings, and we can't put much fuel aboard because I need the plane to be as light as possible."

Josh knew that if the plane did not get airborne, Rusty and Jim would go down in the Yukon. The end of the runway ended at a cliff on the edge of the river. David had already volunteered to stay with Josh to try to find his father, so that had eliminated approximately one hundred and seventy pounds of weight. David had decided that Diana was either dead or lost forever. So, in spite of his sadness about Diana, David decided that at least he could try to help Josh save his father, as some measure of comfort for the crisis that Diana had created for them.

By the time Jim was placed in the plane, fuel was onboard, and the flares were in place, it was almost four o'clock in the afternoon. Rusty had called his wife to inform her of his plans, and that he would need an ambulance at the Anchorage airport. At the end of the grass airstrip, he turned on his landing lights, which was the signal for Josh and David to light the flares. Running from one flare to the next, they managed to light the last flare before the first flares burned out.

Josh and David heard the roar of the little single-engine Cessna as it started toward them. They never actually saw the plane, but they could see its landing lights through the snow. Utilizing the Doppler Principle, they could hear the engine as it came closer and closer to them, and then began to fade away. And then, apparently just before reaching the edge of the cliff, the plane lifted off the ground. Soon the sound of the engine disappeared. Because they did not hear a crash or see an explosion, they felt fairly comfortable that the Cessna was airborne. David offered his hand to Josh and said, "Well done. Thanks for everything that you have done. Now, let's go find your father."

Dawn came around five o'clock, in spite of the heavy cloud cover. The light filtered under the bridge and awakened Tom. The fire had gone out during the night. He was surprised and delighted that he was still alive and well, and that no wild animal had approached him during the night. He craved a warm cup of coffee with some hot chocolate, the beverage they had named Kenai Koffee. Instead, he ate one of the remaining granola bars, and scooped up some fresh snow to melt in his mouth to relieve his thirst.

Compared to being fully exposed to the elements, it was rather cozy under the bridge. Tom was tempted to build another fire, get back into his sleeping bag, and stay there. But knowing how little food he had left, and given the fact that it was getting colder, with threatening skies, he made himself strap his sleeping bag back onto his day pack and get moving again.

In addition to worry about the worsening weather, Tom was concerned that Jim might be in serious condition, and that the snowstorm had prevented an air rescue. He also worried that Josh and his canoe mates might not have made it back to Eagle. Even if Josh had reached Eagle, the storm would hinder his ability to get anyone to come up the highway to pick him up. By his estimates, Eagle was somewhere between twenty-five and thirty-five miles away. Most of the distance was downhill, as he recalled, but there was one steep climb up to about twenty-five hundred feet above sea-level before the last downhill grade. He knew that he had to get up that grade before his strength ran out.

The next eight or ten miles of his forced hike were really almost peaceful. There was no vehicular traffic on the road because of the heavy snow, and it was very quiet. All that he could hear was the crunching sounds of his boots on the snow and ice. Of course, he would have welcomed the noise of a snowmobile, but that did not seem to be in the offing. Knowing Josh's strength and wisdom, his gut instincts made him feel quite certain that Josh and his canoe mates must have reached Eagle by now, but he was still worried about them.

Realizing that he had not urinated in several hours, he stopped and scooped up two handfuls of snow to drink, to try to prevent dehydration. He was beginning to feel considerable hunger. His legs were beginning to feel fatigue, although the rest of his body was not especially tired. He smiled when he rubbed the beard that he had grown, and appreciated the protection that it had given his face. During some of the climbs up embankments along the Fortymile River, there were moments when he would experience an intense burning pain beneath his sternum with heavy breathing, which he attributed to the cold air he was inhaling. His face had been telling him for two hours that the temperature was dropping, but he had not wanted to think about it. Now, he looked at the thermometer on his watch. It was eight degrees above zero He realized then that he had better pick up the pace, mostly out of fear of what the future weather might bring.

Ahead, Tom could see that the road sloped downward around a sharp curve, with a stream far below. He was especially happy that the snow had stopped for a while. If there had been poor visibility, he could easily have fallen off the cliff beside the road. In the distance, the road apparently crossed the stream, and then climbed up, presumably to the high plateau that he had remembered from their trip in the van from Eagle to Dawson.

When he reached the bridge over the small stream, he swallowed more snow to stay hydrated, and rested on the guardrail on one side of the bridge. He was afraid to sit down, for fear that he would not want to get up. After about ten minutes, he began the slow ascent of the Chicken to Eagle road up to the plateau. At about the same time, it began to snow again quite heavily. The snow made it very difficult to see more than a few yards ahead. He concentrated on the road, and tried to stay in the middle.

As Tom climbed higher, he began to get recurrent spells of intense burning in the middle of his chest. The pains abated almost instantly when he would stop walking. He also began to experience considerable shortness of breath. That puzzled him because he had just recently undergone a treadmill EKG, which was perfectly normal. He had been exercising on exercise bikes, the treadmill, and the elliptical machine for months in preparation for the trip. He also often climbed the eight flights of stairs to his office, all without being especially short of breath. The chest pain and shortness of breath caused him to significantly slow down his pace. Tom finally remembered that he had experienced similar chest pain and shortness of breath when he had climbed an eighteen thousand-foot snow-capped mountain in Colombia at the ripe old age of twenty-three, and the recollection calmed him somewhat. The slower pace and the heavy snowfall did worry Tom, though.

Tom kept going anyway. He trudged on up the hill, until he finally reached the summit. After a rest stop, and melting more snow in his mouth, he followed the road across the plateau. The road on top of the plateau must have been two miles, or, at least it seemed so. At long last, Tom felt the road angle slightly downward. The light was beginning to diminish. Tom knew that he should begin to look for some sort of shelter. He began to wish for the comfort of the bridge over the Fortymile, which was many miles behind him. The road was following along a stream, with high cliffs on the side of the road opposite the stream.

Tom searched for an overhanging cliff, and he soon found one that would give him some protection from the falling snow. With darkness rapidly approaching, he frantically scoured the edge of the roadbed near the stream, gathering enough firewood to last for a windy, cold night. When he collected enough wood, he built two small fires near each side of his sleeping bag. He piled extra firewood next to each fire, so that he could reach it during the night without having to get out of the sleeping bag. Finally, he crawled into his sleeping bag without even eating anything, and zipped the hood over his head. In spite of the hardships that he had endured, he felt rather proud of himself for having survived thus far. He had begun to feel a creeping confidence that he was going to make it back to Eagle. It was almost a feeling of bliss; and he fell sound asleep.

After Rusty and Jim had taken off, Josh and David turned to the problem of trying to find Josh's dad. During their earlier visit to Eagle, Josh had seen several snowmobiles. They decided to go to every house where there was a snowmobile parked to ask for help. They approached four houses, and the reply on each occasion was essentially the same: "You've got to be crazy to think I'd go out in this blizzard."

Josh started to panic.

David said, "Let's go back to the cabin, warm up, and think this out."

"Warm up!" Josh replied. "My dad is out there somewhere, probably freezing to death because of your stupid wife."

"Okay, calm down, let's stand out here in the snow and think." At that moment, there was a mournful howl from one of the Malamute huskies in a dog pen around the corner from the Amundsen cabin.

"I know!" Josh exclaimed.

"What?"

"I'll get that guy with the huskies to hitch up his team with a sled."

"Okay, let's go talk to him."

After repeated knocks on the door of the house, a large brawny, bearded man reeking of Canadian whisky came out. He was the same man that Josh and his dad had found so amusing because the crack between his buttocks had been visible when sitting on the bench at the store during their initial visit to Eagle.

"What in the hell do you want?" he said in a gruff, unfriendly voice.

Josh explained the situation, standing on the stoop of the house, with the man blocking the doorway.

"How much are you willing to pay me?"

"Is five hundred dollars enough?"

"In this weather? You've got to be kidding."

"How about one thousand?" Josh said, thankful that his father had given him a thousand dollars back at the Fortymile campsite.

"I guess so, but it's too dark to leave now. I'll take you in the morning, but be here at six o'clock, and bring some food and water and whiskey, if you have some."

On their way back to the Amundsen cabin, feeling disappointed and disillusioned, Josh recalled, to his amazement, some lines from *A Moveable Feast*, his favorite Ernest Hemingway book: "You expected to be sad in the fall. Part of you died each year when the leaves fell from the trees. And their branches were bare against the wind and the cold, wintry light. But you knew there would always be the spring, as you knew the river would flow again after it was frozen."

David said, "Josh, you've done all that you can tonight. We need to find something to eat here in the cabin, so we'll have strength tomorrow. How about some pancakes for supper?"

"Great idea. Hey, by the way, thanks for staying with me."

"No problem," David replied.

At around 5:30 AM, Tom was awakened by a bright light, which startled him. When he unzipped the hood of his sleeping bag, he realized to his amazement and delight that the bright light was sunlight. The snow had finally stopped. Before he even crawled out of the sleeping bag, he tried to find his sunglasses, but the search was fruitless. He assumed that he must have left them in the camp at Fortymile, or else they had fallen out of his day pack. Now instead of not being able to see because of the snowfall, he was having trouble seeing because of the bright, white snow on the ground. He ate his last granola bar, and swallowed some snow to wash it down. He then tied his sleeping bag back onto his day pack, after brushing off the snow, and hoped that this would be the last time that he had to do that. And once again, he started down the road toward Eagle.

Josh and David were at the house of the rough and ready dog driver before dawn. David handed the man a half-empty bottle of rye whisky that he had found in a cabinet in the cabin, from which the man immediately took a swig, wiping the whisky off of his mustache when he finished. "Good enough," he growled. The man was in the process of harnessing the dogs, and attaching the harness to a sled. "I can't take but one of you," he barked, almost like one of the huskies.

"Okay, I'll go," Josh said.

David understandably agreed and said, "I'll be waiting in the cabin. Good luck."

The big man ordered Josh to lie down on the sled, and to hang onto the sides.

"Where do I put the water and these granola bars?" Josh asked.

"Here, I'll take 'em," the man said as he placed them into a bag attached to the back of the sled. He then opened the gate of the dog-pen, quickly jumped on the back runners of the sled, and actually yelled, "Mush!" The big lead dog, which Josh and his dad had seen at an earlier time, standing on its dog house and howling, now let out a long howl, which the other dogs answered, and they were on their way. The dog driver had to hold them back to conserve their energy. The dogs were so glad to go out for a run that they wanted to fly. Josh was very happy that the blizzard had stopped, but he was concerned about the bitter cold. However, the thrill of the sled ride and the thought that they might find Tom alive took away any other concerns.

Tom kept trudging along at a pace that was slower than he had hoped, partly because the white snow on the road was blinding in the bright sunlight. Then there was a more compelling reason for him to slow down: the ever-increasing chest pain and shortness of breath. The thought that he might be experiencing angina pectoris began to settle in, and he even wondered if he had had a myocardial infarction. He knew that ideally he should rest, but with the temperature down to eight degrees, he was concerned that he might freeze to death. His sleeping bag was guaranteed down to minus twenty degrees, and he possibly could crawl into it and wait, but he was out of food, and he did not know how long it would take for someone to find him.

He trudged on. At least the slope of the road was downhill, so he figured that he must be fairly near to Eagle, perhaps as close as five or six miles, if he was lucky. He reminded himself that Roald Amundsen and his three companions had walked and sledded for five hundred miles from Herschel Island on the Arctic Ocean to reach Eagle one hundred years earlier, in the middle of the winter. So, surely, he could walk a few more miles.

Another two or three hours passed, and Tom approached a slight incline in the road ahead. When he reached the top, he could tell that the road again sloped downward, but because of the bright sun on the snow, he could not see anything in the distance. He realized that he might be developing snow blindness. He was exhausted. Since he was on the crest of the little hill, he decided that he had to lie down for a while. Just in case a snowmobile should be out on the road, he laid his sleeping bag down on the side of the road, and zipped it up over his head.

Shortly after lying down, he began to hear the howls of wolves. At first the sounds were in the distance, but then they grew closer. He tried to get out of the sleeping bag, but he was too tired. He began to consider what it must be like to be eaten by a pack of wolves. He wondered if he should expose his neck to the wolves, so that they could kill him quickly without too much suffering. The howling then stopped. Tom heard nothing for fifteen to twenty seconds. Then, even though his sleeping bag was covering his head, he could tell that animals were near him. He peeked out of the sleeping bag, and faced two large eyes and a large nose, with frightful teeth showing. Then the animal licked his face. About that time a man picked him up, sleeping bag and all, and hugged him. He said, "Dad, would you like a lift?"

Another man, whose breath smelled like cheap whisky, helped Josh lift Tom, and they carried him to the sled and covered him with blankets.

After the sled and the dog team were turned around, Josh climbed into the sled with Tom and held him. The sled began to glide over the hard-packed snow. All Tom could hear was the crunching sound of the sled runners on the snow, the soft rhythmic panting of the huskies, and an occasional bark from the lead dog. He was not quite sure if he was fantasizing or if this was actually happening. Whatever it was, it was a happy feeling.

When the sled reached Eagle an hour later, David and Rusty were waiting in the cabin. Rusty had flown in as soon as he had heard that the skies had cleared. He had attached skies to the landing gear before leaving Anchorage. After a cup of coffee and hot chocolate, Josh and David helped Tom walk to the plane. Josh and David sat in the back two seats, and Tom was placed in the seat next to Rusty. As they took off from the little airstrip, Tom glanced down at the mighty Yukon below them, now partly frozen. He thought about two of his favorite lines from Norman Maclean's famous novella: "Stories of life are often more like rivers than books," and, "Eventually, all things merge into one, and a river runs through it."

Their flight path took them to the south of Denali, which allowed them to see the magnificent snow covered mountain in all its glory in the distance to the north. As they neared the Anchorage air space, the flight controller directed Rusty to fly south, and then to land in a northerly direction. This allowed them an amazing view of the Kennicut Glacier as it wound between the high mountains of the Wrangell-St. Elias National Park. As Tom dozed off, he smiled as he thought of a verse from Robert Service's poem, "The Spell of the Yukon:"

There's a land where the mountains are nameless,

And the rivers all run God knows where;

There are lives that are erring and aimless,

And deaths that just hang by a hair;

There are hardships that nobody reckons;

There are valleys unpeopled and still;

There's a land—oh, it beckons and beckons,

And I want to go back—and I will.

PART 2

SIXTY-FOUR SOUTH

"And through the drifts the snowy clifts
    Did send a dismal sheen:
    Nor shapes of men nor beasts we ken—
    The ice was all between.
The ice was here, the ice was there,
    The ice was all around:
    It cracked and growled, and roared and howled,
    Like noises in a swound!"

    From Samuel Taylor Coleridge, "The Rime of the Ancient Mariner"

May 2006

64°7' S, 64°0' W

The last container was being hoisted aboard *Richard Byrd* from the primitive dock at Palmer Station on Anvers Island, one of the few large islands in the Antarctic Peninsula. Palmer Station was the smaller of the two U.S. research stations in Antarctica. The two hundred thirty-foot *Richard Byrd* was a supply-passenger-research vessel plying the waters of the legendary Drake Passage between Punta Arenas, Chile, and Palmer Station. The twenty-eight returning scientists and their assistants had boarded the ship, and all of their gear had been stowed. Since it was May, theirs would be the last ship to depart from Palmer Station for Punta Arenas before ice froze the harbor solid, and daylight essentially disappeared for several weeks.

Antarctica would rapidly become colder as the sunlight diminished, with the temperature on the Antarctic Peninsula averaging from five degrees Fahrenheit to thirty-one degrees below zero in the winter. Twelve hardy souls were staying for the austral winter. They were assisting the deck crew with loading the container by holding onto the container with restraining ropes to keep the forty-knot wind from slinging it into the side of the ship.

Captain Robert Matthews was watching the operation with some degree of anxiety from the aft window of the bridge when the satellite phone rang. He thought, *This is a hell of a time for someone to call.* Robert was in a hurry to get going back to Punta Arenas. He was also dreading the one-thousand-mile crossing of Drake Passage from Antarctica to Cape Horn, undoubtedly the roughest body of water on the globe.

First Mate Cecil Danos answered the phone. "It's for you, sir. She says that it's urgent."

Urgent, Robert thought, *and a she. Oh, shit! It must be my ex- wife. In her opinion, everything is urgent.* "Hello, this is Captain Matthews," Robert said curtly, with barely controlled irritation in his voice.

"Robert, this is Elizabeth McIlhenny, on the *Peary.*" The research vessel Peary was the two hundred seventy-five-foot sister ship that served the same function as Robert's command, except that the vessel traveled between New Zealand and McMurdo Sound, the larger of the two U.S. research stations. Elizabeth McIlhenny was a research assistant on *Peary.*

"Okay, Liz. What's so urgent and why are you calling instead of one of the officers?"

"Robert, we've got a major problem. A glacier calved right on top of the *Peary.*"

"You've got to be kidding. I've never heard of such a thing."

"Believe me, it's true, and we're in a mess."

"What about the crew?"

"The captains are dead."

"Both of them?" Robert asked.

"I'm afraid so."

"How about the mates?"

"One has a broken leg and the other appears to have had a concussion."

"Liz, I'm going to have to ask you to talk with Cecil Danos, my first mate, while I watch this container come on board the *Byrd*."

Captain Matthews knew that he needed some time to think. He also needed to make sure that the container was secured properly to the aft deck. There was a forecast of a major storm approaching from the west, heading straight toward Drake Passage, and Matthews knew that winds along the coast of Antarctica frequently reached one hundred miles per hour during the winter.

The container of garbage going back to Chile from Palmer Station was at that moment swinging wildly back and forth in the strong wind. One of the shore crew at the station had slipped on the icy dock and dropped the restraining line, thus releasing the container. Finally, one of the crewmen on *Byrd* ran across the narrow gangplank and grabbed the flailing rope. He took control of the container just before it smashed into the base of the crane that was lifting the container. The container was then gently lowered onto the aft deck and secured to the waiting brackets.

"Okay," Robert said, turning to Cecil. "What's going on aboard the *Peary*?"

"Captain, I think you should hear the story from her yourself, if you don't mind."

Puzzled, Captain Matthews picked up the phone. "Okay, Liz, I'm back. Now, tell me more."

"Well, as I said, a glacier calved right on top of us. We were doing some undersea soil sampling next to the glacier, hoping to find fossils that might have come down with the glacier. When the glacial fragment fell onto the ship, the ship listed to port approximately thirty degrees and went flying down the inlet where we were for at least a mile. There was no way to stop the vessel. The bridge was crushed onto the 03-deck beneath the bridge. We figure that the officer on the bridge and the captain sleeping on the 03-deck were killed instantly. It took us quite a while to dig the two mates and the two captains from underneath the ice, so it is possible that the captains may have lived for a while underneath the ice and the wreckage of the bridge. It took us several hours to saw, chip, and blowtorch the ice from the ship."

"What about the chief engineer and the rest of the crew?" Robert asked.

"They're all okay."

"And the scientists and their assistants?"

"All okay, too."

"Are the engines functioning?" Robert asked.

"Yes and no. The engines are running, so we have power, but the falling ice hit the steering wheel on the bridge, so there is no way to steer the vessel."

"Do you have an anchor out?"

"Yes."

"Where are you calling from?"

"The forward part of the 01-deck, up near the bow. This is the only place that I could get the satellite phone to work, since its antenna has to be in an open space."

"Okay, let me think a minute. By the way, Liz, where is the *Peary*?"

"In Marguerite Bay."

"What's the air temperature?"

"It's about twenty degrees Fahrenheit," Liz said.

"How about the water temperature?"

"The last time that I looked at the gauge on the bridge was about an hour or so before the glacier calved on us. The water temp was twenty-five degrees."

"Isn't it getting rather icy there?"

"Yes, and I was getting worried about that, but my boss insisted that we finish the soil sampling before leaving. That's when the calving took place."

"Okay, honey, we're coming to get you. I don't know how long it will take us to get to you because I don't know the extent or thickness of the ice in your area, but tell everyone on board that we're coming and to stay calm. We've got to take care of a few things here before we can leave, but that shouldn't take long. When I call back, I will need to talk with the chief engineer and the medic, as well as the chef. I'll call you when we get under way."

"Thanks."

"Did you say that you were calling from the bow?"

"Yes."

"Well, I don't want you to be standing out there in that wind and cold, waiting on my call. So how about you calling us back in roughly an hour?"

"Okay"

Robert turned back to the large window in the back of the bridge on the starboard side that overlooked the cargo deck. *Marguerite Bay*, he thought. He had a vague recollection of where it was, but he had never been there. Over the ship's public address system, Robert yelled, "Hold everything!" Then, trying to calm his voice, he announced, "Don't tie down that container. We have a problem. Rather, the *Peary* has a problem. I want that container to go back to the dock. Now! I'll explain why when that gets done."

After the container had been placed back on the dock, Robert turned on the intercom for the entire ship. He assumed his most professional command voice and said, "Let me have your attention. There is a crisis on the *Peary*. We need to go to her aid immediately. I want all scientists and their assistants to immediately exit the ship and return to Palmer Station with their belongings. As soon as that last container has been secured on land, I want all of the crew of the *Byrd* to board ship and prepare for immediate departure. I know many of you will be very disappointed to not be returning home after spending so much time in Antarctica, but we need your space on board this vessel to bring home your colleagues on the *Peary*, some of whom may be injured.

Robert paused, took a deep breath, and continued speaking. "Let me explain. The *Peary* has been struck by a calving glacier, and has been badly damaged and incapacitated. They are several hundred miles to the southwest of us, and we need to get to them ASAP. We will only have space on this vessel for essential crew members, so that we can ensure that there's enough space aboard for the scientists and crew members from the *Peary*. At this point, we know that both captains have been killed and the two mates have been injured. As far as we know, none of your fellow scientists have been killed or injured."

Robert paused again and tried to relax a bit. *Marguerite Bay*, he thought. *I must get to a chart.* He resumed speaking over the intercom. "I need for Doctor McClamrock to come up here to the bridge. Also, I need to speak with the chef and the chief engineer. In addition, I need for both mates and the alternate captain to come to the bridge. Mr. Chief Engineer, we will need full tanks. This may be a long voyage. That's it for now. Get cracking everyone. We've got to get under way soon!"

"Marguerite Bay. Marguerite Bay," Robert said aloud as he switched off the ship's intercom. *This is my chance to look it up,* he thought. The large slanted table covered with navigation charts was on the other side of the bridge, to the port side of the wheel. He quickly crossed over to the chart table from where he had been standing on the starboard aft side of the bridge. He hurriedly lifted the charts lying on the table until he found the chart with an overview of the Antarctic Peninsula. Remembering that Marguerite Bay was somewhere southwest of Adelaide Island, he found it quickly, and then he made a rough estimate of how far it was from their current position.

Palmer Station was at sixty-four degrees south latitude, and Marguerite Bay was at sixty-eight degrees south latitude, but approximately one degree of longitude more westerly than Palmer Station. Thus, Robert estimated that *Peary* must be between two hundred forty and three hundred nautical miles southwest of them, and ninety miles south of the Antarctic Circle. If his ship could maintain its usual cruising speed of twenty knots, they could reach *Peary* in twelve to fifteen hours. However, with ice rapidly forming and a strong storm heading straight toward them from exactly where they had to go, they would be lucky to make ten knots. Also, darkness was already upon them, even though it was only three o'clock in the afternoon, which meant that they would have to slow down to look for icebergs.

"Captain, what can I do for you?" Tom McClamrock asked, his soft Southern drawl obvious.

Tom had just gotten back aboard the ship after making one last sortie out to the edge of the glacier behind Palmer Station to watch the glacier calve. When *Byrd* had first arrived at the station, Tom had borrowed some poles and crampons, and climbed the five hundred feet to the crest of the gently sloping glacier. The view from the top was amazing. High purple and black mountain peaks projecting above the white glaciers could be seen for at least fifty miles.

"Doc, I know you came on this trip as the company's guest, but now I need your help." For over thirty years, Tom had been the physician for the Louisiana family whose company built and owned *Byrd* and *Peary*. He was also the physician for many of the company officers and captains. Robert went on to say, "As you probably have heard, our sister ship, the *Peary*, is in trouble. We know of at least two deaths and one serious injury. There may be more. We are going to their aid, and I need you to go with us."

"Not a problem," Tom replied. "I will just need to use the satellite phone to call my wife and my office."

"Good. Get one of the mates to show you how to use the phone, but make it brief because I will be needing the phone to call the *Peary*."

Tom turned to leave the bridge. "Hey, Doc," Robert yelled after him. "I know that this is messing up your practice back home in New Orleans, but thanks."

"Don't even think about it. This will be kinda fun. By now, you must know that I like a little adventure in my life."

Tom had instantly liked Robert Matthews. The captain was quiet and rather serious, but pleasant. In fact, Captain Matthews had served as the captain on a catamaran that ran back and forth between Eagle, Alaska, and Dawson City in the Yukon. When Tom and his son had canoed the Yukon, they had seen the catamaran pass several times. The vessel would always slow down, so as to not create a wake that could capsize their canoes. Matthews was well educated and urbane. He had an air of success and authority, which gave him an appearance of a CEO. In addition, he was lean, fit, and handsome, with close-cropped dark brown hair that was graying at the temples. He had piercing bright blue eyes that seemed to bore into anyone he talked to.

During the trip across Drake Passage from Chile to the Antarctic Peninsula, Tom would often climb up to the bridge to look out for whales and icebergs. In fact, as *Byrd* was leaving the Straits of Magellan and entering the South Atlantic, Tom had had a moment when he wondered to himself what in the world he was doing, and he had briefly considered jumping on board the Chilean pilot's boat before it pulled away. At that very moment, about thirty white bottle-nosed dolphins with black coloration on their faces began to dance and jump behind the ship, with that remarkable smile that only dolphins have, and Tom decided that all was going to be okay. Tom was accustomed to the black dolphins with white markings found in the Gulf of Mexico. They often cavorted behind the sailboat that he and his son sailed together.

When Robert was at *Byrd*'s helm, he often played classical music on his CD player. Robert also knew by heart all of Robert Service's poems, such as "The Cremation of Sam Magee." On one such night, Tom told Robert about his trek from the Yukon River campsite on the Fortymile River, and up the Fortymile to the road to Eagle. Robert told Tom that the trip was probably twice as long as he had estimated, more like fifty miles.

As Tom began his descent down the steep stairs of the bridge, he ran into the alternate captain, whose name was Sam Adams, the two mates, and the chief engineer. "The captain is waiting for you," Tom said, as if they didn't know that. "When one of you has a moment, I need someone to show me how to use the satellite phone."

"Will do," replied Cecil Danos.

On the bridge, Robert quickly got down to business. "First of all, do we have enough fuel to go perhaps two hundred fifty nautical miles south and then back?"

"Yes, sir. We have enough for that and to get us back to Punta Arenas," replied the chief engineer.

"What if we get stuck in the ice?"

"That's a question that I cannot answer. It depends on how long we might be jammed in the ice, and on how much fuel might be expended in getting us out of the ice if we did get locked in."

"I understand," Robert said. "Okay, we need to get going. I'm counting on you two mates. Plus you, Sam, to help me make sure that everything possible is ready for an evacuation and return, either back here, or straight to Punta Arenas, once we find the *Peary*. In the meantime, we will need to set up shifts, as usual, until we get to Marguerite Bay. Captain Adams, I will leave it up to you to set up the duty shifts. Also, captain, I am asking you to serve as our weather officer because advance warning of the storm's progress will be crucial to us. That's all for now. Thanks. Oh, by the way, I'll take the first watch until you get everything set up."

The men turned to go, but Robert stopped them and asked, "One more thing, do any of the crew wish to stay behind here at Palmer Station? After all, this is not really what they signed on for, and it is possible that we could get marooned."

"They all want to go, sir." Sam said.

"Good. Then let's clear the dock and get going." Robert went back to the microphone at the aft window of the bridge. "Deck crew. Is everything secure? Okay. Pull up the gangplank and cast off the lines. Let's get going!"

The big diesel engines had been purring for several hours, but now they revved up a bit in anticipation of an impending departure, almost as if they knew instinctively, like a well-trained dog, that the master was about to move out. When the last lines from the bow and stern were cast off simultaneously, the ship sidled away from the dock.

Arthur Harbor on Anvers Island was hardly what one would call a harbor in the usual sense of the word. It was more of a narrow inlet off the bay to the southwest of the island. The scientists who had been forced to disembark and those who were remaining behind for the austral winter were standing in a long line on the dock, but not a single person waved. The sadness was palpable. Likewise, no one on *Byrd* waved or said anything.

As the ship began to pull away from the dock, Captain Matthews turned on the three huge searchlights located above the bridge. The lights cut through the darkness of the winter afternoon. Robert gently pushed the throttle forward to give the ship a little more speed, and he took the vessel out of Arthur Harbor into the open water. The amount of ice that had coalesced since they had arrived stunned him. Although the ice was thin, the presence of so much was a sign that winter was upon them. They would have to hurry if they were going to reach *Peary* before the ship was locked into such thick winter ice that *Byrd* could not get through it to reach the stricken ship and rescue the people on board.

Tom returned to the bridge after making his calls and said, "Captain, I'm shocked at the amount of ice formation."

Robert said, "Doc, since you're a scientist, you probably would like to know what I know about sea ice formation."

"I certainly would. Please tell me."

"Okay," Robert said. "Well, sea ice in the Antarctic region begins as crystals about an inch long. As the darkness deepens, the crystals coalesce into pancakes, and then into floes of greater and greater size. The floes freeze together and become thicker and deeper, until the ice reaches an average thickness of three feet. The ice forms incredibly fast at a rate of twenty-three square miles per minute. By October, at the end of the austral winter, the size of Antarctica will have doubled."

"Absolutely amazing!" Tom said.

There was a slight sound of movement in the aft part of the bridge.

"Captain, do you mind if I stay on the bridge with you for a while?" said a man with a deep Cajun accent.

"Sure, but remember you will be up here by yourself sometime later tonight, and you will want to be rested and ready."

"Roger that. I agree, but I have never been in Antarctic waters at night with so much ice."

"Doc, you know Mike Boudreaux, don't you?"

"Sure."

Robert thought that it really might be a good idea for the inexperienced mate, Mike Boudreaux, to observe for a while. On the way south from Punta Arenas and the Straits of Magellan, he had only been assigned to the helm during daylight hours once they had reached the ice. Also, even when they had encountered ice, it was mostly large icebergs and the smaller bergs called growlers. Growlers were named from the famous poem by Samuel Taylor Coleridge, where he talked about how the ice growled.

"Phone's ringing. Will you get it, Mike?" Robert asked.

"It's for you, sir."

"Captain Matthews here. Is that you, Liz?"

"Yes."

"You sound like you are very cold. Are you okay?"

"I guess so."

"How is the mate with the concussion?"

"He's coming around, but he is still confused about where he is."

"Well, tell the chief engineer that he is in command, and don't let that mate give orders to anybody or do anything. How about the mate with the leg fracture? Did the medic put the leg in a splint?"

"Yes, but I'm worried about him. He looks very pale and weak."

"I'll get our doctor to talk with you about him. Make sure that he is warm, in case he is getting shocky. Anybody else injured?"

Tom interjected, "Captain, you have told her all that I would have said."

"No."

"What have you done with the bodies of the two captains?"

"We laid them in a long tool chest on the forward deck, near where I am standing. We figured that the cold air would keep their bodies preserved."

"Right. Good thinking. By the way, our doctor tells me that you are doing everything that he knows for you to do for the mate with the leg fracture," Robert said. "Okay, let me tell you where we are. We have just left Palmer Station, and, at this moment, we are heading out toward the open ocean on a southwesterly course from the southwestern tip of Anvers Island toward the Briscoe Islands. We will stay out at sea to avoid the sea ice until we reach Adelaide Island. We will then need you to give us your exact position, so we will know what course to take to find you in Marguerite Bay. There is no point in giving us your exact position at this time. By the way, I'll call company headquarters to report what's going on. Tell everyone to stay calm. We're on our way. We should be there in twelve to fifteen hours."

"Right. Do you want me to call you in another hour?"

"If you can, please do so. At that time, ask the chief engineer to call me and give me your approximate location. Oh, and by the way, tell everyone to pack his or her gear and to be ready to transfer to *Byrd* as soon as we arrive. We don't want to be delayed by anyone because they have not packed."

"Gotcha."

After an hour and a half of cruising, Robert said, "Mike, round up the other two officers, plus the chief engineer, and ask them to join us up here."

"Roger that, Captain," Mike responded in his best U.S. Navy form. After twelve years on active duty, mostly at sea, Mike still reacted to commands from ranking officers as if he was still in the service. Robert stared ahead though the darkness, frequently glancing at the radar screen. He knew that icebergs could suddenly appear out of the fog and mist, and require immediate attention to avoid a collision.

"We're all here, Captain," Sam Adams, the alternate captain, said in a soft, quiet, and calm voice.

"Good, that was quick," said Robert in a pleased tone of voice.

"What's up?" asked Adams.

"Well, I thought it might be wise to pool our thoughts before we go too far, and also to prepare the crew for what may be ahead."

"Excellent idea," said Adams.

"Okay, why don't you tell us what you are thinking first," chimed in Danos, one of the mates.

"Very well, then." Captain Matthews spoke slowly and deliberately. "As I see it, we should continue on this current course toward the west-northwest until we get clear of the Antarctic Peninsula, and south of Hugo Island. If all of you will follow along with me on the chart, I believe you will have a better understanding of my thoughts."

Sam Adams, Mike Boudreaux, and Cecil Danos gathered around the chart table to study the chart. Tom McClamrock respectfully stayed out of the way, since navigation was obviously not his forte.

Robert continued, "Then we should turn to the south-southwest well offshore to avoid the ice. With the approaching storm, we probably will get our brains beaten out. Nevertheless, I think we can make better time in open water, rather than trying to feel our way through the pack ice, and dodging icebergs and those pesky tiny islands that you can't see until the last minute. Also, that narrow channel between Adelaide Island and the Arrowsmith Peninsula is probably already slammed shut with ice, or it soon will be. Once we get past Adelaide Island, we can then turn back toward the mainland into Marguerite Bay, and try to find *Peary*. Those are my ideas, but I would be interested in your ideas or suggestions."

"Everything you say makes sense to me," said Captain Adams, who was several years older than Robert.

Every vessel in the company had redundancy built into its key systems, such as the engines, and into its key personnel positions, such as the commanding officers. Robert just happened to be the commanding captain and Sam Adams the alternate captain on this particular voyage. On another trip, it might have been just the opposite. Adams grew up in Massachusetts and was the grandson of a major seafaring shipping magnate, but before he was of age, the grandfather went bankrupt during the Great Depression prior to World War II.

Sam was tall, about six feet two inches in height. He had a very broad chest and broad shoulders, and a bit of a potbelly from too many good meals and wine. One of his favorite sayings was that he had never had a bad meal or a bad glass of wine. Sam flunked out of Harvard at the end of his freshman year, because he found out that there were thirty girls' colleges in the area around Boston. After that, he joined the U.S. Air Force, where he served as a navigator on the old C-124 transport planes. He was always cheerful and jolly, and a great raconteur.

The two mates did not dare to say anything, now that the two senior officers had spoken. In addition, neither of them had any ideas that were better than those already expressed.

"However," Adams went on, "I do think that we should start making some contingency plans in case the ice is too thick in Marguerite Bay for us to reach the *Peary*. You two mates might want to put your education to work, and see if you can come up with some alternate plans in case we need them."

Both mates simultaneously said, "Yes, sir."

"Doc, you probably don't know this, but this vessel is not an icebreaker like the *Peary*. The *Byrd* is ice capable, but she's not an icebreaker," said Captain Adams.

"Hmm," Tom McClamrock said, almost to himself. "I seem to recall that a Belgian expedition to Antarctica became stuck in the ice for several months in the late 1800s. In fact, Roald Amundsen was on the voyage, and he learned a lot from that experience that helped him later get to the South Pole first, before Scott."

"You are correct, Doc," said First Mate Cecil Danos, "and where they were frozen in place is roughly where we are headed."

"Gentlemen, let's keep those facts to this group of us here on the bridge. We don't want to create any more anxiety among the crew than probably exists already," Robert said. "All right, those of you who are not on duty should get some rest." Robert turned away from them to give his full attention to steering, as he stared out through the windows into the darkness and frequently glanced at the radar screen. The last thing that he needed was for them to collide with an iceberg or a *nunatak*, one of the miniature mountains that poke up through the ice and the glaciers along the coast of Antarctica.

"One more thing, Sam," Robert said. "Before you leave the bridge, please call the office in Louisiana, and tell them what has happened and what we are planning to do. Also, we need some instructions from them about what to do with the *Peary*, since I'm sure that they don't want the *Peary* to be salvaged by another country or another company."

Tom McClamrock climbed up into the top bunk in his cabin. He had been sharing the cabin with one of the scientists, until all of the scientists and their associates were suddenly expelled from the ship because of the accident on *Peary*. The scientist had had a hip replacement, so Tom had volunteered to take the top bunk. Since he felt certain that the crew had not had time to change the bed sheets, he went ahead and climbed into the top bunk. His mind began to race as he thought of what they might encounter when the reached *Peary*, and of what might be expected of him. He also thought about the fact that the privilege of taking this voyage had turned into a mission that he had not imagined in his wildest dreams. He did not expect to be able to sleep. However, the gentle swaying of the vessel and the soft purr of the big diesel engines soon made sleep irresistible.

At around 2:00 AM, Tom felt the telltale urge to urinate. As he began to slowly and carefully descend from the top bunk, a sudden powerful wave hit the vessel broadside on the starboard beam, and the vessel heaved violently to port. At that moment, Tom was flung straight out from the bunk, like Peter Pan, about four feet in the air. For a brief moment, he was at zero gravity, like an astronaut in space, until gravity grabbed him and brought him crashing to the deck of the cabin. Fortunately, he landed on his buttocks and his right elbow. Except for an abrasion on his elbow, he was unscathed.

After he finally was able to stumble and crawl to the toilet and complete his mission, he decided that he should put on his pants, and go up to the bridge, one floor above, to see what was happening. While he was in the toilet, he had quickly realized that urinating from a standing position, as was the usual male practice, was impossible with the violent lurching of the vessel from side to side. Even sitting on the toilet was a challenge.

"Welcome back to the Southern Ocean," a cheery, slightly sarcastic voice said as Tom opened the door to the bridge. Captain Adams was at the helm, and he turned only for a second to look at Tom. He kept his eyes focused on the radar and what view he could see through the ice and salt on the windows of the bridge. "We are obviously outside of the protection of the islands now, Doc. You okay, Doc?"

"Yeah, I think so. I just took a flight out of the top bunk, but I'm okay."

"Damn, Doc, you could have really gotten hurt. Move into the bottom bunk immediately. Also, take the bag that holds your lifesaving gear, and stuff it under the side of your mattress, so that your mattress tilts you toward the bulkhead. That way you won't roll out with a big wave."

"Gotcha," Tom said,

"Hey, Doc, you're a colon specialist, huh?"

"That's right," Tom replied.

"Well, Doc, there's a giant petrel down here that puts out fifteen pounds of stool a day."

"You've got to kidding me!" Tom said.

"Nope. In fact, one of the scientists at Palmer Station is studying that pile of stool. I'm sorry that you didn't meet her. You could have taken a picture of one of those piles of shit and framed it and hung it on the wall of your office. Then, when someone came to you complaining of diarrhea or constipation, you could have pointed to the photo and said, 'and you think you have a problem!'"

Tom roared with laughter, until he thought that his ribs might break.

On the way south from across Drake Passage, the ship passed through the turbulent waters of the so-called Polar Front, where the warm waters of the South Atlantic Ocean and the South Pacific Ocean collide with the frigid waters of the Southern Ocean. The convergence of these warm and cold waters, and the unrelenting west winds, make Drake Passage very rough almost all the time. The passage was named for Sir Francis Drake, the famous explorer, pirate, and protégé of Queen Elizabeth the First. Tom had not experienced seas like these. Tom recalled that when Drake entered the Pacific Ocean after passing through the Straits of Magellan, his sailing vessel, which was then named *Pelican*, but was later renamed *Golden Hind*, got pushed back into the passage that now bore Drake's name. Drake was finally able to sail on up the west coast of South and North America to discover San Francisco Bay.

To avoid a broadside wave like the one that threw Tom across the cabin, Captain Adams had now turned the vessel directly into the wind and waves. The anemometer on the top of the bridge was registering wind speeds of ninety to one hundred knots, the equal of one hundred fifteen to one hundred twenty-five miles per hour, or a Class 3 hurricane. The bridge was fifty feet above sea level, and the waves were crashing over the top of it. The vessel would never make it to the crest of an oncoming wave before it would crash through and go down into another deep trough. Tom began to wonder how long the ship could stand the punishment, but, to his amazement, he felt no fear whatsoever. He was very puzzled by this peculiar peace of mind. He was not sure whether it was because of his faith in God, or whether he had confidence in the captains, or whether he had subconsciously decided that there was no advantage in worrying at that point in time.

"What`s going on?" a sleepy voice said. It was Cecil Danos. Right behind him was the other mate, Michael Boudreaux. Both mates were from the French-Cajun area of south Louisiana. Danos was small in stature and dark haired, like the typical Frenchman, whereas Boudreaux was larger and more muscular, but with the same French characteristics.

"Come on in and enjoy the ride," said Captain Adams. "I have a marvelous sense of well-being."

"What! You must be crazy to like this kind of weather!" said Mike Boudreaux.

"You mean to say that this rocking and rolling keeps you young guys from sleeping? If you plan to stay up here, how about doing some charting for me? I haven't been able to record our position for over an hour because of this rolling."

"Okay," Danos replied, "where are we?"

"Look it up yourself, son. You should know how to read a GPS," Sam replied smartly. "I've got my hands full here at the helm."

"The GPS says that we are exactly at sixty-five degrees south and sixty-six degrees west, which puts us at about one hundred nautical miles due north of the northern tip of Renaud Island, one of the Briscoe Island chain."

"Okay, mark it on the chart," Sam said curtly.

Tom had read about the discovery of Renaud Island by the French Antarctic Expedition, and he was intrigued by the fact that the expedition was led by Jean-Baptiste Charcot, a physician who had turned explorer. He was the son of a very famous French physician, who had described a constellation of symptoms of a biliary tract problem, so named Charcot's Triad. Tom was struck by the coincidence that another physician who had turned explorer, Dr. Frederick Cook, was on the *Belgica* voyage that became locked in the ice.

"How long do you plan to maintain this course?" asked Boudreaux.

"Don't know yet," Sam replied. "But I have to keep the bow headed into these waves, or the rolling could be too much for the ship to handle."

"Well, we can't go too far out into the open ocean, or we'll have a hell of a time getting back into Marguerite Bay," a voice from the back of the room said quietly.

"Welcome to the party, Robert," Sam said politely. "I was just teaching these fellows how to fly a ship."

"Well, I believe that we are going to have to give up my plans to go outside," Robert said. "Instead, I believe that we should turn back to the southeast, and go behind Renaud Island to get on the lee side of the island. Hopefully, in the next ten to twelve hours, the wind will die down and we can venture back outside." Robert spoke with authority, indicating that he had made up his mind.

"I agree," Sam said. "But get ready for a pounding on the starboard side when we turn to port."

Slowly and painfully for the two captains, the ship turned to port. As the vessel turned, the waves from the northwest hit her broadsided, and she listed at a forty-five degree angle for what seemed like fifteen minutes, but it was probably more like fifteen seconds. Everyone on the bridge, except for Captain Adams, who was holding onto the wheel, slid and fell across the room into the portside bulkhead. Finally, *Byrd* slowly righted herself, but then sustained another fierce blow to the starboard side, throwing her once again onto a forty-five-degree tilt.

"I don't have anything to hold onto, so I'm going to bed," Tom said as he half-crawled to the door.

Robert then said, "Why don't you two mates do the same, and be ready to take the helm later. Sam and I will alternate at the helm until we get out of this rough weather."

"Aye, aye, Captain," they both said simultaneously.

Tom had great difficulty descending from the bridge down the steep stairs because of the lurching of the ship. He finally made it to his stateroom, and crawled to the toilet. He did not dare to stand to urinate. He crawled back to the bottom bunk, managed to stuff the lifesaving outfit under the mattress, and climbed into the bunk with his clothes on. In spite of the violent motion of the ship from port to starboard and back, the rocking brought sleep almost instantly.

Tom awoke at precisely 6:00 AM, his usual time. When he stood up, he immediately noticed that the vessel was not lurching. In fact, the ride was the smoothest that he had felt throughout the voyage. There was a new faint sound of swishing or crunching, which he had never heard on the ship before, but it reminded him of the sound of the till from glaciers rubbing on the bottom of a metal canoe as it moved through the water. He had heard that same sound while canoeing on the Yukon River two years earlier. It also brought back memories from his high school English class, when he had had to memorize parts of Coleridge's famous poem, "The Rime of the Ancient Mariner," where the poet described the ice as growling. He pulled on his shoes and once again climbed up to the bridge. To his amazement, there was a brilliant white seascape everywhere, as far as he could see, even though there was very little daylight. *Ice*, he thought.

"There is a great breakfast downstairs in the galley, Doc," said Cecil Danos from the helm. "You might want to eat well, since this could be a long day."

"Will do, thanks."

When Tom reached the galley four decks below the helm, he was greeted with the sight of nearly the entire crew.

"Welcome to breakfast, Doc," said Sam Adams.

"Thanks, and good morning to everybody," Tom replied. "I like this ride much better."

"So do we," several said in concert.

Tom then proceeded to load his plate with pancakes, fried eggs, and bacon, plus a large biscuit. After he had placed his tray on a table, he went back to get orange juice, coffee, and water. "We must be on the leeward side of Renaud Island, judging by the smooth ride," Tom said to Captain Matthews.

"Right."

"So far the ice is only one foot thick," chimed in Captain Adams, "but we won't be able to handle it if it gets much thicker."

"That's why these guys are pushing my lady so hard," added the chief engineer.

"I was thinking that we were going rather fast, but I thought maybe it was the effect of the ice on the hull," Tom said as he wolfed down his breakfast.

Robert Matthews whispered to the group of officers sitting together, "Let's get off this subject. Remember, essentially the whole crew is in the room."

"Right," said Sam.

When Tom got up to get a refill of his coffee, he realized that without the scientists and their assistants, there really were not a lot of people on board. There were two captains, two mates, two engineers, a chef, a dishwasher and preparer of the food, one steward to keep the cabins clean and the beds made, two deckhands, and Tom, the guest of the company. "Wow," Tom thought. "This is one hell of a trip."

Tom went back to his cabin to brush his teeth and use the toilet. While he was in the cabin, he remembered that he had brought along a copy of Dr. Frederick Cook's book about the *Belgica* expedition. The book described the austral winter of 1898 to 1890, when *Belgica*'s crew were trapped in the ice. It was similar to what had happened to *Endurance*, Ernest Shakleton's famous ship. Roald Amundsen, who later became the first explorer to reach the South Pole, was also on the *Belgica*. To Tom's amazement, and somewhat to his alarm, they were roughly following the same route that *Belgica* had taken on its ill-fated cruise.

Thanks to the ingenious idea of Dr. Cook of having the crew eat raw seal and penguin meat to prevent scurvy, most of the expedition members survived. British sailors had established that scurvy could be prevented by consuming juice from limes, lemons, and oranges. Hence the term Limey was applied to British sailors. The British sailors had seen the good of drinking citrus juice long before it was known that it was the vitamin C in these fruits that was the protective agent against scurvy. Obviously, citrus fruits did not exist in Antarctica.

When Tom went back up to the bridge, he could feel the tension. Captain Matthews had decided after breakfast in a private conversation with Captain Adams that there should be both a captain and a mate on the bridge at all times. The channel through the small islands between the Arrowsmith Peninsula and Adelaide Island, the last large island in the Palmer Archipelago, was extremely narrow. In addition, there were numerous icebergs of various sizes in the channel, which meant that the ship had to weave around the bergs, sometimes putting the vessel dangerously close to the shore.

Captain Adams and Captain Matthews appeared to be having a conversation when he arrived. Tom said, "Do you want me to leave you two alone?"

"No," they both replied simultaneously. "Sam was just telling me that our boss wants us to somehow maintain a presence on the *Peary* to prevent salvage by another vessel from another country," Robert said.

"You may or may not know that once a vessel has been abandoned in international waters, it is legally fair game for salvage by any vessel," Sam went on to explain. "Furthermore, there is some very sensitive equipment aboard the *Peary*, as well as on this ship, that we would not want to fall into other people's hands."

Tom did not respond, but he began to wonder what they meant by "sensitive equipment." He had noticed numerous tall transmission towers behind the Palmer Station base buildings, and he thought that it was unusual for a research station to have so many communication towers, but, since he had never been to a polar research station, he assumed that the towers were standard.

After six hours, they reached Marguerite Bay. Robert called Liz. "Okay, Liz, we're here," he said. "Now, tell us where you are."

"Thank God you're here."

"Are you able to give us your position?"

"Sure. it is exactly at sixty-eight degrees south and sixty-eight degrees west."

"Wow! That makes it nice and easy. We will head your way. In about two hours, I may ask you to turn on your searchlights to help us see you. The last thing we need is a collision."

"Right."

"Okay, why don't you go back inside and get warm, and then call in one hour."

"Roger"

By now, both captains and both mates were on the bridge. "Need a break?" Captain Adams volunteered.

"Not yet, but I may want to take a leak soon. I'll let you know," Robert replied.

Silence. The apprehension could be felt. Part of the anxiety was created by the fact that sometimes the radar would pick up icebergs that could not be seen in the thick fog that had settled in. Although it was fortunate that radar could detect the bergs, the crew knew that not all bergs could be detected by radar. Robert said, "Okay, Sam, take over for a while, but I would feel better if I stayed up here."

"Not a problem," Sam replied.

Robert said, "I'm going to the head, and then I'm going to make some fresh coffee."

"What speed do you want us to maintain, Robert?" Sam said over his shoulder.

"Let's cut it to five knots until this fog lifts, if it ever does, Sam."

Another hour passed. The phone jarred them out of their trance, the ring seeming exceptionally loud. First Mate Danos answered the phone. "Is that you, Liz? Has it already been an hour?"

"You're right on both occasions," she replied.

"Tell her to turn on the three searchlights, with the center one pointing roughly in a southeasterly direction, and the other two splayed out in a slightly different direction," Sam ordered.

"Will do," Danos said.

"I could hear him over the phone," Liz said quickly. "I'll get it done and call back in another hour. Okay?"

"Okay."

Silence again. All was quiet, except for the sound of the ever increasingly thick ice scraping alongside the hull of the ship.

Thirty-five minutes later, Sam yelled, "Shit!"

"Hard to port!" yelled Robert from the back of the bridge, spilling the coffee that he had made earlier all over his shirt. "Stop engines!"

Peary was directly in front of them. The sideways motion of *Byrd* slowed the forward progression of the vessel, but there still could have been a collision if there had not been such thick ice surrounding *Peary*. Instead, the two vessels slowly and gently slid closer and closer to each other until they touched. The connection resembled the smooth docking of a space shuttle into a space station, instead of the potentially disastrous collision that almost occurred.

By this time, *Peary*'s crew was out on deck with lines ready to heave onto *Byrd*. The vessels were secured with the starboard side of the aft deck of *Peary* across from the port side of the aft deck of *Byrd*. For the time being and under the present circumstances, it was a good arrangement. However, Captain Matthews immediately became concerned that because of his order to turn to port, the disabled vessel was the one facing out to the open sea, and his vessel was facing toward the mainland of Antarctica, with the ice growing thicker and thicker by the minute.

Robert realized that he had to get *Byrd* turned around so that it faced out toward the open ocean as soon as possible. But he first had to transfer the scientists and crew from *Peary* to *Byrd*. For a fleeting moment, Robert mused on the thought that the vessel named for Admiral Richard Byrd, the famous American explorer of Antarctica, was attempting to rescue the crew of a vessel named for an equally famous American explorer of the Arctic, Admiral Robert Peary. He then asked Captain Adams to remain on the bridge, while he scrambled down the outside ladder aft of the bridge to the deck just above the working deck. Speaking over the handheld loudspeaker, he said, "Okay, let's place our gangplank onto their deck." When the gangplank was in place, he climbed down to the working deck and started across the gangplank.

Tom was watching all of this from the walkway around the bridge. By the time Robert had reached the halfway point of the gangplank, all of the crew and scientists aboard *Peary* were out on their working deck, some with their travel gear in their hands. Spontaneous applause broke out, stopping Robert in his tracks. He raised his arms and waved for them to stop. "Look, we're just glad that we could get here to pick you up. You would have done the same for us. Now, I want all of you scientists and your assistants to get your stuff and get aboard the *Byrd*. Our two mates will help you find quarters. We are down to a skeleton crew, so there should be plenty of room, although I doubt if anyone will have a private cabin. Now, I need to meet with the crew of the *Peary* in the galley of your ship. Doc, would you go check on the two injured mates, and then join us in the galley?"

"Will do. Would someone show me where they are?"

A tall, handsome, but not stunningly beautiful woman with dirty-blond hair stepped forward. She had a somewhat muscular build, a deep tan, and looked like she was probably forty to forty-five years old. "I'll show you," she said with a crisp Scottish burr.

"You must be Liz," Tom said.

"Right, and what's your name?"

"Tom McClamrock."

"Scottish?"

"By ancestry. Not native born."

"I could tell that by your accent."

"Of course."

Silence.

"My father is a cardiovascular surgeon," she said, breaking the awkward silence.

"No kidding. Where?"

"Edinburgh, but we live in a little hamlet at the end of the Firth of Forth."

"I know the area. It's on the way from Edinburgh to St. Andrews."

"Precisely. Do you know the UK?"

"Some. I trained for a while in London, and on weekends my wife and I zipped around the countryside. I particularly liked Hadrian's Wall. To me, the Wall epitomizes the Scots. Too tough for the Romans, so the Romans had to build a wall to keep them out."

She chuckled, nodding.

"Well, here we are in the ship's infirmary. This is Joe, the ship's medic."

"Glad you are here, Doctor. I need your help," the medic said. He was a healthy-looking young man was sitting in a chair in one corner of the room. He put down the book he was holding and said, "This is William Robichaux, the mate who sustained a concussion. He still has some loss of recent memory, but he seems to be doing okay. This is John Beatrous, the one with the broken leg. I splinted it according to the instruction book, and I have been able to keep him out of pain with Percocet, but he is very weak."

"Let's look at the leg," said Tom.

The entire leg was swollen and dark blue, indicating an obvious massive amount of bleeding into the leg from the fracture site. The leg was also very cold. "What was his last blood pressure and pulse reading?"

"Pulse of one hundred twenty and BP of eighty over forty."

"Fever?"

"No, sir."

"It looks like he must have lost four to five units of blood into that leg. From what you have told me, plus the swelling of the thigh, I'd say this obviously looks like a closed fracture of the femur. Therefore, his leg really needs to be in traction. Also, we need to tilt his head down and put him in a Trendelenburg position. We need to give him a couple of bottles of D5 half-normal saline or Ringer's lactate to get him out of shock. Can you handle that, or do you need me to help you?"

"I can do it, sir."

"Good. Come find me if you need me."

"Right."

"By the way, make sure that he stays warm."

"Yes, sir."

"Okay, doctor, I guess that we should join up with the others in the galley," Liz said

"Right," Tom said.

They climbed down to the galley where *Peary*'s crew was seated in a row on a bench at a long table facing Robert Matthews. Robert turned as they entered and said, "Come on in. Gentlemen, this is Doctor McClamrock. Liz, I was just explaining to the crew that the company wants us to maintain a presence on the *Peary* until the vessel can be repaired or towed to Punta Arenas. The chief engineer and the chef have already volunteered to stay."

The chief engineer, Ramos Fuera, was a very large and tall man, with a rather "rough around the edges" look that perhaps stemmed from the fact that he was a very heavy drinker when ashore. He talked a lot and very loudly, probably because of the loneliness of the engine room and his deafness, which was caused by the diesel engines. No one called him by his real name. Instead, everyone always called him chief.

The chef, Manuel, was a very small and slight man from Chile. He was very quiet and somewhat humble in appearance, was an excellent cook, and very creative in his menu choices. He also had a knack for making some devilishly delicious chocolate-chip cookies.

Robert said, "We should not need a full crew, since we will not be under way. I plan to stay on board, and send Captain Adams in command of the *Byrd*. I am going to ask one of our mates on the *Byrd* to also stay. Doc, can the two injured mates travel?"

Tom thoughtfully responded with deliberate slowness. "The guy with the concussion is okay to travel, but someone needs to make sure that he is helped when climbing the ship's ladders. However, the other guy has a serious fracture. If we should hit the kind of waves that we encountered on the way here, that could be disastrous for him. Therefore, he has to stay here. I'll stay to take care of him, and the medic can go on home."

"Are you sure?" Robert asked.

"I'm sure."

Actually, Tom was not so sure that he wanted to stay aboard *Peary*. He didn't relish the idea of possibly spending several months in darkness and the cold, but he felt that as a physician he couldn't desert the man with the broken leg. Also, he surmised that Robert Matthews would feel a lot better with a physician aboard. Tom figured that he might as well assume his practice in New Orleans would be finished if he didn't return to New Orleans within a month.

After looking at Tom straight in the eye for a few seconds, Robert said with a smile. "Okay. It really will be nice to have a doctor on board."

"What about you, Liz?" Robert asked.

"You know that I have to stay, Robert," Liz replied.

"Yes, I know. It will also be nice to have you around, too," Robert said with a slight smile.

"Thanks," Liz said.

"Okay then. Let's get our gear aboard the *Peary*," Robert said as he indicated by his departure that the meeting was over.

While Robert Matthews was gathering his gear, he had an impromptu meeting in his cabin with Captain Adams and the two mates, Danos and Boudreaux. Boudreaux volunteered to stay with Robert on *Peary* since he was single, and, quite frankly, was looking forward to the experience. Danos had a wife and two children. Even though Danos was more experienced, Robert had a strong feeling that Boudreaux would fit in better, perhaps because of his military discipline. Robert knew that he was going to miss the companionship and wisdom of Sam Adams. Sam was always upbeat and positive in his thinking, in addition to having a wonderful sense of humor.

The four of them then talked about the fact that the ice might have coalesced around the two vessels, even though *Byrd* had only been stopped for an hour or so. They decided to use the bow thrusters to try to pry the ships apart. If necessary, they would send some of the crew out onto the ice with the firefighting axes to break up the ice around *Byrd*, so they could turn the vessel around and point the bow toward the open water of the Southern Ocean. In case any of the crew should fall into the frigid water while hacking at the ice, they decided to tie a line around the crewman's waist with another crewman holding the other end of the line. That decided, Matthews and Boudreaux bid farewell to Adams and Danos, and climbed back on board *Peary*.

Byrd's engines had not been turned off, so the ship was ready to go immediately. Lines between the two vessels were cast off. The crews stood on the working decks, with the captains and mates on the bridges. Interestingly, none of the scientists and their assistants came out on deck. Tom McClamrock thought that this was strange; it puzzled him. He thought that out of respect for their rescue, they would have come out on deck to wave good-bye. He decided that perhaps they were embarrassed, or that maybe they just wanted to stay out of the way.

Using the starboard bow thruster, Captain Adams was able to push *Byrd*'s port side with sufficient force that the ice gave way, and he was then able to turn the vessel slowly and ever so carefully in a semicircle until the bow faced toward the open water in the distance. Fortunately, the ice floes were still loosely knitted together, even though the ice was now one to two feet thick. Then, at a speed of three knots, the ship pulled away from *Peary*, leaving behind six men and one woman to fend for themselves.

For more than an hour, Robert, Tom, Mike Boudreaux, and Liz silently watched the departing vessel, until it was no longer in view. The chief engineer and the chef were drinking coffee in the galley and had no desire to watch *Byrd*'s departure. Robert pushed the control button that electronically pulled the anchor back inside the hull of the ship. *Peary* would now drift with the sea ice, just like *Belgica* had done over a hundred years earlier. Robert made a mental note to record their position every twenty-four hours, mainly out of curiosity, so as to record their drift. The darkness of the austral winter had closed in on them.

It was three o'clock in the afternoon, and it was already dark. The sky was overcast, so there was no moonlight, no starlight, and not even any light from the aurora australis, the Antarctic equivalent of the aurora borealis, the Northern Lights of the Arctic. Robert called for a meeting of everyone in the galley to get organized for the winter lockdown. He first asked Manuel, the chef, to outline his plans for meals and conservation of the available food on board. Manuel was confident that, given the small number of people on the ship, there would be enough food to last for several months. The kitchen pantry had been stocked with enough food to accommodate a larger number of crew and scientists.

Tom piped in with a warning. "Let's try to conserve enough orange juice among ourselves to prevent depletion because of the importance of preventing scurvy," he said, remembering *Belgica*'s voyage again. He also urged everyone to share vitamins if some people did not have them.

Robert then said, "Everyone will be expected to keep their respective cabins clean and neat, and to wash their own bed sheets and towels and clothes, and to empty their own trashcans."

All agreed that this was reasonable. Robert also reminded everyone that there was an exercise room on board, and that he expected everyone to use it at least three times a week, and preferably more often. If anyone wanted to take a stroll out on the ice, it was imperative that they let him know when they were going and when they returned. In addition, he said that people going outside the vessel must follow the buddy system.

The chef announced, "Breakfast will be at 7:00 AM, lunch at noon, and dinner at 6:00 PM. The galley will be open at all times."

Thus, all those aboard settled down for the long austral night. The quietness and the darkness were strange and eerie and somewhat unnerving. Before retiring to his cabin for a while, Tom decided that he should check on Robichaux, the injured mate. One plastic container of fluid was almost empty, so Tom hung up the second container. The young man did not acknowledge Tom's inquiry as to how he was feeling.

There was a frosty looking material around the man's mouth that fit the description of uremic frost, but Tom had never seen it himself since no patient in today's civilized world would be allowed to reach that stage of renal failure. Tom surmised that the man had not been urinating much, and that his kidneys were shutting down. Tom then checked the mate's blood pressure, and was alarmed that it was fifty over twenty in both arms. He tilted the bed into a steeper Trendelenburg position, as much as could be allowed, considering that the leg traction had to be maintained. The man did not appear to be in any pain, but his respirations were very shallow and irregular. Tom decided that he should let Captain Matthews know about the mate's condition, and then climbed back up to the bridge. The two of them came back down to the infirmary. Tom could not feel a pulse, and the man's pupils were dilated and fixed.

Robert said, "Is he gone?"

"I'm afraid so," Tom said. He released the traction on the leg, and he and Robert picked up the mate and put him in the outside locker with the two dead captains. For a brief moment, Tom reflected to himself, "Maybe I should have stayed on the *Byrd*, now that Robichaux is dead."

Both Tom and Robert had carried the mate to his "coffin" on the deck without putting on coats and gloves. In the five or ten minutes that they were outside, their faces and hands had become numb. They realized how stupid that they had been to go out so unprotected, but, at least, it got their minds off the thoughts of the death of such a young person.

The next day was the Fourth of July. It would be one of the darkest days that they had experienced. The darkness added to their sense of isolation and loneliness. Even though U.S. Coast Guard regulations forbade alcohol consumption on U.S. vessels, Captain Matthews brought out a bottle of Pisco wine to share for dinner that night. He had purchased it in Chile. He decided that since they were not in motion and since it was a national holiday, he would bend the rules a bit. Manuel was from Chile, and he volunteered to make Pisco sours for everyone.

Tom had loved Pisco sours since a trip he had made to the Machu Picchu as a young man. He said, "I'd like to make the first toast to Chile and to Manuel for these wonderful Pisco sours." The little group then made toasts to the American Revolutionaries, and to the American explorers of the Arctic and the Antarctic.

They all knew that they should get into a routine, in order to keep their health and sanity. Breakfast was attended by all. Robert would have already used the gym and had showered and shaved each day before breakfast. The engineer and the chef said that they did not need to exercise. Robert and Tom visited with them together, and urged them to do so, but they felt that they got enough exercise in their daily activities. Liz exercised after breakfast and then "fixed herself up." Tom and Mike Boudreaux exercised at various times in the afternoon. Also, on days when it was not snowing or foggy, Tom, Mike, Liz, and Robert would go for hikes across the ice to try to find something interesting, and to break the monotony.

The only wildlife they saw were the ever-present birds, especially the skua and the albatrosses. They were too far from the open water to see seals. Besides, the leopard seals could be vicious and tear off a man's leg. The penguins had long ago gone to the mainland of Antarctica for the winter. In the evenings, there were plenty of books in the library and movies on CD to watch. It was also a time to send e-mail messages home, and to receive them. So the days and weeks began to pass by.

Once a week, Liz went out a short distance from the vessel to make some sort of scientific observations, which she did not discuss. She went by herself, but always arranged for someone to watch her from the vessel. At other times, several of the group would take hikes out onto the ice, always making sure that someone was on the ship to receive messages and to turn on the searchlights, in case darkness caught them out on the ice. The window of opportunity for these walks on the ice was very brief, usually only two or three hours between 11:00 AM and 2:00 PM.

Robert asked Mike, "Whenever any of us go out on the ice, would you be responsible for informing Chief and Manuel?"

"Certainly, sir. You can count on it."

On one of the sorties out onto the ice, Tom asked, "Robert and Liz, how long have you known each other?" It was apparent that they were friends.

Robert said nothing, but Liz said, "We go back a long way." An awkward silence followed, a silence that puzzled Tom.

Robert quickly said, "We'd better get back to the ship before it gets darker."

It was very apparent to Tom that Liz and Robert knew each other very, very well.

As time passed, everyone's schedule became less rigid. In fact, so many people began to sleep through breakfast the Robert and the chef declared that there would be no prepared breakfast, in order to save food. Instead, there would be juice, milk, coffee, bread, and yogurt always available for those who wanted it. Lunch was moved into brunch, so that anyone who wished could go outside during the daylight hours.

Tom and Mike continued to use the gym in the afternoons. To keep up their spirits, they often would also go for a walk on the ice in the mornings, especially on sunny days. One day, Tom asked Mike, "What do Mutt and Jeff do during the daytime?"

"Who?" Mike asked quizzically.

"Chief and Manuel," replied Tom. "You're too young to remember the comic program about Mutt and Jeff. I can't even remember whether it was a comic strip, a movie, or a TV series, it's been so long. Anyhow, it was a funny story about two guys, one big and one little, who were friends."

Mike chuckled. "Well, I don't really know what they do, but I often see them sitting in the kitchen playing cards or just talking. They seem to have developed a friendship."

"Okay," Tom said. "Well, I guess that by the nature of their inside jobs, they don't have any interest in being outside."

"I guess so," Mike replied, "However, if it was me working in the kitchen or in the engine room all day, I would be craving the outside."

"I agree," Tom said.

Robert realized that he might as well sleep a bit later, so he began to exercise in the morning with Liz. Liz exercised in a jogging halter and short-shorts. Robert was amazed at the six-pack of her abdominal muscles. Even though there did not appear to be an ounce of body fat on her arms or thighs, her breasts were still large and stretching the material in her halter. Once, when she caught him looking at her, she said, "You still have an eye for me, don't you?"

He said, "Humph. Well, I couldn't help but notice. After all, I'm a man." Nothing more was said. Shortly after that, Robert left to take a shower. Liz followed him to his cabin, and he answered the knock on his door wearing only his gym shorts.

She appeared to be angry, which made her look even sexier to Robert. She putting her hands on her hips and asked, "What happened to us?"

"What do you mean, what happened to us? What happened to you? You disappeared that day that I went to make a call in Hvar, and I never heard from you again, until you called me down here in Antarctica."

She started to cry. "Didn't you know?"

"Know what?"

"The Serbs took me. Six or seven of them grabbed me from our boat and took me to Split on the Dalmatian Coast."

There was silence for a long moment before Liz continued. "They gang raped me so many times on the boat ride that I passed out. Then they left me strung up naked in a barn somewhere in the mountains. I would have died from hypothermia if a group of Bosnian and Dutch soldiers had not found me. I was in a hospital in the Netherlands for a month."

"I'm sorry. I didn't know." Robert said softly, with his head bowed. Liz turned on her heels and left, letting the door slam behind her.

Robert sat down in a chair and covered his face with his hands in despair. After a short time, he crawled into his bunk, lay back on his back, and reflected on their time together in the former Yugoslavia.

They had met in Dubrovnik at a bar overlooking the Adriatic Sea. He had captained a ship loaded with arms and ammunition for the Bosnian-Croatian Army during the height of the conflict between

Bosnia, Croatia, and Serbia. They had fallen instantly in love. He had never known why she was in Croatia. She had told him that she was a freelance writer, but he did not believe her. He was so wildly in love with her that he did not care if she was telling him the truth or not. They chartered a sailboat and sailed along the Dalmatian Coast to Hvar, an island that caters to nudists. They spent most of their time on the sailboat sun bathing nude on the foredeck, with occasional breaks to make love. Occasionally, they went into the little town to buy food or wine.

One day, a motor launch passed near their sailboat. Liz glanced at the men in the boat and felt a chill. Robert noticed her reaction, but said nothing about it. The next night, Robert said, "I have to go into town to the little hotel to make a long-distance call to my boss in the States. I'll be right back."

"Want me to go with you?" Liz asked.

"No, this won't take long," Robert replied.

He recalled that as he was walking back to the dock after his phone call, taking a shortcut down an alley, someone clubbed him from behind. When he awakened, he was surprised that his billfold was still in his pocket, along with his passport. When he reached the sailboat, Liz was gone. He walked the streets of the town all of the next day and night looking for her, but to no avail. He finally sailed back to Dubrovnik alone, in deep depression. The American consulate in Dubrovnik was no help, either because they were too preoccupied with the conflict, or, as he suspected, they did not want to help him.

Now, as he reflected back on it, he realized that the Serbians must have suspected that Liz was a secret agent working for the Bosnian-Croatian cause, and that she had arranged for the shipment of arms and ammunition that he had brought in on his ship. At the time that they met, Robert was tall, very vigorous, and a quite strikingly handsome thirty-something-year-old man with a cosmopolitan air, which he had acquired from his experiences in traveling all over the world. He had been married once, but his years at sea had soured that relationship. Now he was turning grey, and he did not have such bravado as he had exhibited a few years earlier. He was still strikingly handsome and tall, but much quieter and more reclusive. He exhibited even more confidence than in the past. Women found him very attractive, but he had never married again.

One day at lunch several days later, Chief was eating at one end of a table with Manuel. As Mike had told Tom, the chief engineer and the chef had become buddies of a sort, since they did not exercise or take strolls on the ice like the others. Tom, Liz, Mike Boudreaux, and Robert were eating at the other end of the table. Tom asked Liz, "What had you been studying in Marguerite Bay when the iceberg calved on top of the *Peary*?"

She paused thoughtfully before speaking, like a pipe smoker packing his tobacco, and replied, "As you may or may not know, fossils of ferns and whole trees have just recently been found by British scientists in the Fossil Bluff area of Alexander Island, which is just southwest of us. Since the *Peary* could not reach the shore of Alexander Island because of the ice, we were collecting soil samples from the ocean floor as close as we could to the island, looking for more such fossils. That is when the calving of the glacier took place."

"Fascinating," Tom replied. "So this shows that perhaps Antarctica was part of a rain forest, either in the tropics or a temperate zone. Correct?"

"Correct. In fact, there is a theory that Antarctica may have been connected to the area of British Columbia and Alaska," Liz said.

Robert listened to this explanation with interest, but said nothing. Tom suspected that Robert did not believe Liz's story was the whole truth, but it was just a nagging feeling. Enthusiastic about the fossils, Tom went back to his books in his cabin to read more about

Alexander Island. He discovered that it was originally discovered in 1821 by the great Russian Antarctic explorer, Admiral Thaddeus Bellinghausen, for whom the sea in which they found themselves was named. The island was named for Czar Alexander the First. Great Britain now claims it under the Antarctic Treaty.

Tom put down his book, distracted with the notion that something was not right between Robert and Liz. He had noticed a certain aloofness between them during the past few days, which puzzled him. Of course, with not much else to do, it was easy for everyone to study the words and the body language of everyone else, and to then make judgments, right or wrong, about what was going on.

After that conversation at lunch, it seemed to Tom that Liz spent more and more time in her cabin. Her absence was noticeable since she was the only woman on board, and especially because she was good looking and was becoming even better looking as the days wore on. Robert and Tom happened to be out on the ice one day by themselves, since no one else wanted to go. Tom said, "Robert, what's going on with Liz? Is she getting depressed or cabin fever?"

"No, I think that she's okay. Don't worry about her."

"Okay, whatever you say. You seem to know her pretty well," Tom said, somewhat sarcastically.

"That's right, we used to have a thing going a long time ago," Robert said softly and somewhat sadly.

Tom quietly and respectfully said, "I see."

One evening, Robert couldn't stand the separation from Liz any longer, so he knocked on her cabin door after dinner. She invited him in. She was dressed in tight-fitting Patagonia long underwear, which she customarily wore as sleepwear. "What's on your mind?" she said.

"Well, I came over to ask you some more about your research work, but, after looking at you in your underwear, I have other things on my mind," he said.

"Would you like for me to take off my underwear?" she said in a rather haughty manner.

"Sure, if you are inclined to do so," replied Robert, puzzled that she would do this in such a cold-mannered way, with apparent hostility.

"Well, you'll have to take off your clothes also," she said, again with deliberate coldness in her manner.

"Okay, that's easy," he said, beginning to wonder if he really wanted to have sex with her now, or, for that matter, if he could make love to her. It seemed to him that she was trying to punish him in some bizarre way.

They took off their clothes and stood there naked, awkwardly facing each other. She lay down in her bed and motioned for him to join her under the covers. She gently began to caress him, until he in turn began to caress her breasts, and began to kiss her mouth and all over her body. She could feel that his penis was erect against her body. When she felt that he was ready, she pulled him toward her. Not wanting to take complete control of the situation, she let him slowly enter and withdraw his penis from inside her, until they could not resist the urge to give way to their passion and ultimately reached climax.

"Now, I can answer your question about the other research that I have been doing," she said as she propped herself up on an elbow. "There has been a noticeable increase in the radiation levels in this area of the Antarctic Peninsula lately. For many years, random samples of radiation levels have been taken, mostly because of the loss of the ozone layer in the atmosphere above Antarctica. These radiation levels have been stable for many years, until recently.

That is what I have been doing once a week when I go out alone on the ice."

"Any theories as to why the levels are increasing?" Robert asked.

"Well, interestingly, the U.S. spy satellites have noticed strange longitudinal black lines in the glacier covering Peter the First Island, which is northwest of us about two hundred miles from here. Peter the First Island is claimed by Russia, since Bellinghausen was the first one to discover it. It is basically an impregnable fortress, since it is a volcanic island with sheer cliffs extending straight out of the sea. It is 95 percent glaciated. The only people who have ever seen the center of the island went there by helicopter," she said.

"Okay, tell me more," Robert said

She replied, "You must certainly be aware of the Russian research station on King George Island, at the northeastern end of the Palmer Archipelago."

"Of course."

"As you probably also know, that station has an all-weather harbor which never freezes. Consequently, fairly large supply vessels come and go with impunity. Smaller icebreaking "research" vessels seem to frequently come and go from the base. No one seems to know where these smaller vessels go during the austral winter because of the darkness and the fog, or, for that matter, what they are doing, but we do know that each vessel carries a helicopter. Are you following me?" she asked.

"So far, but what has all of this got to do with the black lines?" Robert asked.

"Robert, you're thinking about sex and not paying attention," Liz said. "Do you remember that I said that Peter the First Island was 95 percent glaciated?"

"Yes," he replied.

"Well, if there are black lines in the glacial ice and snow, what does that tell you?"

"It looks like something must be melting the ice and snow, exposing the underlying black rocks."

"Precisely. Now, what could cause that?" Liz asked with a smug look on her face.

"Something hot." Robert said.

"Of course," Liz said. "Something like used uranium and plutonium rods."

"Oh, shit! You think that the Russians are disposing of radiation waste by dumping the rods on the interior of that island?"

"Exactly."

"Are you married, Liz?" Robert asked from out of the blue.

"Well, by law, yes, but I haven't seen my husband in six or seven months. He's a cardiologist who works with my father. They're both workaholics, and I'm too wild and crazy for either one of them. I'm more like my dead mother."

"I see."

"You still switch subjects in the middle of a conversation, don't you?" she said.

"Yes, I guess so. Does that still irritate you?"

"I don't know. I'll have to think about it. Let's stop talking and make love again."

"Good idea."

As the days passed, Robert spent more and more of his time with Liz. He began to accompany her on her walks out on the ice. On one of their walks together, he brought up the subject of the spent uranium and plutonium rods. "If the rods are still 'hot,' then how do the Russians get them down here without causing radiation injury to the crews of the ships?" asked Robert.

"Well, the theory is that the rods are shipped in protective containers from either Murmansk on the Baltic Sea or Vladivostok on the North Pacific, or both. When the ships with the rods reach the research station on King George Island, the rods are transferred in their protective cases to the smaller research vessels, and then are taken to the area near Peter the First Island during darkness, which, of course, is easy during the austral winter. A helicopter then lifts the hot rods out of their cases by an attached cable, and then drops the rods in the center of the island."

"Very creative. So that's why the radiation levels are rising in this area, since the winds always blow from the west toward the east in this area of Antarctica, and Marguerite Bay is east and south of Peter the First Island."

"Exactly."

"Has any data to support this theory been transmitted to the atomic energy commissions of the United States or the United Kingdom?" asked Robert.

"Some, but we didn't want to tip our hand too soon," Liz replied.

"Who is *we*?" asked Robert.

"I can't tell you."

"Do you think that the Russians suspect that you are on to them?"

"I don't know, but I am worried that they may be suspicious that we are watching them."

"Are you the only one with the data?"

"Yes, it is stored here in the computer files on board the *Peary*."

"Why are you storing it, and not sending it on to whomever you are working for?"

"Good question. We were concerned that anything sent electronically could be intercepted. In fact, we are somewhat concerned that we may have a mole in our communications group."

"Well, don't you think that you should download the files onto a CD, or one of those little chip type things that you put on a key ring, in case something happens to this ship?" Robert asked.

"I agree. You're right."

Two nights later, Robert was up on the bridge checking his e-mails when the satellite phone rang. After a brief period of listening to the person on the other end, he hung up the phone and went to Liz's cabin. When she opened the door, he said, "I just received a call from the States. One of our submarines has apparently been following a Russian sub since it left Murmansk. The Russian sub is now in the Bellinghausen Sea, not too many miles from where we are."

"Oh, shit!" she said. "Who told you this? How do you know that it's true?"

Robert replied, "Believe me, I know that my sources know what they are doing, and this information is true. Who do you really work for?" he asked.

"I said I can't tell you, so don't ask me about it again, okay?" She was beginning to wonder who *he* worked for, and about how he had gotten the information concerning the Russian submarine.

Robert said, "Have you downloaded that information onto a CD or something yet?"

"No, but I will do it right now."

"Good, I think that would be very wise. I'll see you in the morning. Early," Robert said. "Oh, by the way, one of our spy satellites has been commanded to watch the area of Marguerite Bay closely."

Liz said, "Thanks, but I don't think that I will sleep much tonight."

The next morning at breakfast, Robert called an impromptu meeting with all on board. He said, "We have a suspicion that something international is going on that may involve us. I know that that is hard to believe, with our little ship and crew sitting out here stuck in the ice in the Antarctic, but it may be true. Based on some research that has been going on, we may have discovered some information that makes the Russians uncomfortable, and which could embarrass them before the international community. I have a suspicion that we may have some uninvited visitors from an approaching Russian sub in the near future. We will need to make some contingency plans in case that happens."

"What do you mean by contingency plans, sir?" asked Mate Boudreaux.

Robert answered, "I am in the process at this moment of trying to come up with such plans. I will let you know about them ASAP, so that we all will have input. Believe me, you will have a voice in any decisions."

"What makes you think this visit is going to happen, Captain?" said the chief engineer.

"I can't tell you, Chief, but believe me, I have good reason to think it may."

"Okay, I trust you," Chief said.

In his best command voice, Robert said, "Until I can come up with a good plan to put before you, let's go about with our routine as usual as possible. But, doc, I need to talk with you up on the bridge."

"Okay," Tom said.

Liz went to her cabin, leaving the mate, the chief engineer, and the chef sitting together in stunned silence. On the bridge, Robert got right to the point with Tom. "We know that there is a Russian submarine out in the Southern Ocean just beyond the pack ice. I'm sure that you don't know that Liz has discovered a high level of radioactivity in this area, which may be coming from the dumping of radioactive waste by the Russians on a deserted island not far from here."

"You've got to be kidding!" Tom said. The revelation startled him.

"It's true," Robert said. "And, I am just paranoid enough to think that the Russians could be sending a hit team on that sub with orders to blow up our vessel. If it's true, their mission is to destroy any data that may have been obtained to substantiate this suspicion of ours."

"Wow! Okay, so where do I fit in?" said Tom.

"From what you have told me about your experience in the Yukon and Alaska, I know that you know how to survive under such conditions as we find ourselves now."

"Right, but it was not pleasant."

"I'm sure. Nevertheless, I want you to work up a plan to take Liz across the pack ice to Rothera, a British research station located on Adelaide Island. It's about fifty miles northeast of our position. I want you to do this in case we are approached by hostile forces."

"You're dead serious, aren't you?"

"Dead serious, I'm afraid."

"What about the other crew members?"

"I'll handle them."

"Oh, by the way, how did you learn about the Russian submarine?" Tom asked as he prepared to leave.

"Do yourself a favor, and don't ask. Just trust me."

"Okay," Tom said as he headed for his cabin. He was somewhat in a state of shock while he tried to force himself to think about the assignment that had suddenly and unexpectedly been thrust upon him. For a fraction of a second, he allowed himself the luxury of thinking about his wife and children, and he wondered if he would ever see them again. Then he jerked his mind back to the task at hand.

He immediately thought about the fact that there were no sleeping bags or tents on board. However, there were the tightly packed lifesaving suits that were to be used if it was ever necessary to abandon ship. He had had to use one of the units to roll his mattress toward the bulkhead after he was thrown out of the top bunk during rough seas. These suits were especially designed to be waterproof and windproof. They were fitted with a hood. Tom examined the suit and the case in his cabin. He was pleased that the cases had a long strap, which meant that it could be tied around his waist. Liz would have an identical suit. If they had to wear the suits, they would sweat, and the sweat would chill them in the cold temperatures. Combined with the usual long underwear worn by everyone, and shirts, pants, and jackets, Tom figured the clothing would be sufficient to provide for a cover in lieu of a tent or sleeping bag. He would have to check to see if everyone had waterproof boots.

Since potable water was heavy, they could not carry it with them, so they would have to depend on ice and snow for hydration, as he had done in the sub-Arctic. Since there were plenty of granola bars on board, that would have to be their food source. The bars were light in weight, and they did not require cooking. Thus, Tom thought he had a plan. He decided to use the compass on his watch, rather than trying to carry a larger and heavier compass. Realizing that he might have trouble reading the degrees on his watch compass, he figured that he would have to concentrate on gross directions, such as north-northeast, northeast, and so forth. His only concern was the fact that there would be only two people in their party, and he was the only man, even though he surmised that Liz might be stronger that he.

Tom went back up to the bridge to discuss his tentative plans with Robert. "It sounds good to me," Robert said. "Anything else?"

"Yes," Tom replied, somewhat timidly.

"What's that?"

"I think someone else should go with Liz and me."

"Who do you suggest?"

"How about Boudreaux?"

"You're probably correct. Okay, take Boudreaux with you. You probably should inform him."

"Gotcha," Tom said as he headed for the ladder to the lower deck.

"Hey, Doc!" Robert yelled after him. "Nice job. You can do it. I'm counting on you."

"Gotcha, but I'm more worried about you."

"I'll be okay. By the way, let's have a meeting with everyone in the morning after breakfast to bring everybody up to speed."

"Good idea. Good night," said Robert as he headed off for what he suspected would be a sleepless night.

At 3:00 AM, Robert was fitfully trying to sleep when the alarm on his satellite phone went off. He reached for the phone on his night table and turned on the speaker. "Satellite. Seven. Seven thousand meters." *Shit*, Robert thought. *What kind of coded message is this?* Then he realized that whoever had sent the message was aware that it might be intercepted. He decided that a spy satellite had detected a hostile force of seven men approaching *Peary*, and that they were only seven thousand meters away. Robert spoke one word into the speaker: "Rothera." He grabbed his pants, put them on, and began to bang on the doors of every cabin to awaken everyone. "Everyone in the galley! *Now!*" he shouted.

When all hands had gathered in the galley, Robert explained to everyone what he thought was going on. He relayed the cryptic message that he had just received. He said, "Liz has the information that we think the Russians want. Therefore, I have asked Dr. McClamrock to escort her to a location that I prefer to keep secret, just in case we are boarded and that information is requested in an ungentlemanly way. It's in your best interest to not know the answer if asked. I would ask you to tell our guests that Liz, Doc, and Boudreaux left on the *Byrd*. Okay, Doc, it's your show now."

Tom said, "Liz and Michael have already made their preparations. All that we need to do is grab some granola bars and get moving. Liz, I presume that you have the CDs that you need?"

"Right," she said.

Robert said, "Let's turn off all the outside lights right now to make us less visible. Also, all inside lights visible through portholes should be turned off. One more thing, we need to get you a light line to tie to each of you, in case you get separated in the dark."

Chief said, "I'll get the line."

When Liz, Doc, and Mike Boudreaux returned with their supplies and gear, the remaining three members of the crew helped them go over the side of the vessel. Liz was the last to go overboard. She hugged Robert with her head on this chest, and he kissed her lightly on the cheek. He said, "You'd better get going. By the way, I love you."

"I know. The feeling is mutual," she said, and then she disappeared into the darkness.

Robert went back up to the bridge to wait for the intruders. He had tried to reassure Manuel, and to express his appreciation to the chief and the chef for staying with him. About three hours after the others had slipped away from the side of the vessel, he saw flashlights approaching steadily toward the ship.

Chief and Manuel were playing cards in the galley. Robert notified the chief engineer of the approaching Russians, and the two of them grabbed their coats and gloves. They went up on the bow of the ship to watch the approach of the men. As Chief left the galley, he picked up the knife that he had often used to chop vegetables when Manuel needed some help. There was an amazing sense of calmness in both the captain and the chief engineer, perhaps because they knew that they were serving an important purpose.

Robert muttered softly, almost under his breath, "And the sea will grant each man new hope, and sleep brings dreams of home."

"That's nice," Chief said. "Where'd you get that?"

"Christopher Columbus."

"Oh. Were you guys friends?"

Robert chuckled.

When Tom went over *Peary*'s gunwales onto the ice, he was stunned by the blackness of the night. Although he, Mike, and Liz had hiked around on the ice many times in daylight, all three of them were amazed at how difficult it was to walk on the ice in the darkness. They had forgotten how the ice would buckle in places, forming walls and small cliffs. During the day, it was easy to find a passageway around these obstacles, but at night traversing the ice field was very difficult. They soon became exhausted and had to rest.

Looking back toward *Peary*, they could not see the vessel, but they suspected that Robert and the chief engineer had wisely turned off the lights. Tom was very pleased that he had asked Mike to serve as their navigator. Mike assured him that they were still on the north-northeast course that they had agreed upon before leaving the ship. Mike had been very reluctant to leave his captain to accompany them. He only agreed to go with Tom and Liz after Robert convinced him that his mission was more important than if he had stayed with the ship.

Robert suggested to Chief that he make the chef aware of the approaching intruders when they appeared to be about one mile away from the ship. At roughly a distance of two hundred fifty yards, Robert turned on the three searchlights and pointed all three of the lights directly into the faces of the approaching men. Robert knew full well that doing so would probably anger them. The men kept coming directly toward the ship.

Tom, Mike, and Liz clearly saw *Peary*'s searchlights go on, lighting up the darkness in an instant. The three of them estimated that they must be approximately three miles to the north of the ship. Suspecting that the ship was receiving its unwanted visitors made them forget their fatigue, and resume their painful trudge, climb, and crawl to try to distance themselves from the ship. They each had one small flashlight, but none of them dared to use it, for fear of alerting the intruders. Their curiosity and concern for their colleagues on the ship made them want to stop their march toward Rothera, but they knew that they must keep moving.

When the seven Russian men, whom Robert assumed were SEAL-types, reached the area in front of *Peary*'s bow, Robert climbed down on one of the outside ladders to the working deck three decks below, flipping on the light switch for the deck lights as he left the bridge. Three Russians arrived on the starboard side at the same time. Robert peered out into the darkness and said, "What do you fellows want?"

"We want the woman," the commander of the group yelled back in remarkably good English.

"What woman?" Robert replied. "We don't have a woman on board."

"We know that you do because we have intercepted her transmissions, and she signs her messages with Liz."

"Well, she left with our sister ship, the *Byrd*, several weeks ago."

A sudden blow to the middle of his back with the butt of an AK-47 rifle knocked Robert to the deck.

"Now, get up and tell us the truth," one of the men said in broken English. Four of the commandos had climbed aboard the vessel from the port side, while Robert, Chief, and Manuel had been looking ahead at the men standing outside the starboard side of the vessel.

Realizing what might befall them, Manuel said, "I tell you. She ... "

Before Manuel could say anything more, Chief dashed forward, covered Manuel's mouth, and with one swift stroke of his knife, he cut his friend's throat, severing the two jugular veins and the two carotid arteries. Blood sprayed everywhere, soaking Chief's clothing. The Russians opened fire, pumping bullets into his body from several handheld submachine guns. He and Manuel died within a minute of each other. Two commandos picked up Robert and held him while a third slammed the butt of his rifle into his abdomen repeatedly. With a Herculean effort, Robert managed to free himself from one of the men, and slugged the other man. A rifle butt hit him in the back of the head, and he fell unconscious onto the deck.

"You idiot!" yelled the commander of the team in Russian. "He was our chance to find the woman! Okay, let's search the vessel while you two experts set the explosives."

The two explosive experts had brought plastic explosives, which they placed in four critical locations on the inner side of the hull in the engine room, below where they assumed was the waterline. Two of the explosive charges were placed near the place where the fuel lines connected to the engines. They disconnected the fuel lines, so that fuel began to flow onto the floor. Meanwhile, four other men scoured through the rooms containing computers and collected CDs, which they thought might contain damaging information about their country's activities. They left one man to guard the unconscious Robert. Of course, they were also hoping that they might find Liz and any other people on board.

Perhaps the cold Antarctic air revived Robert somewhat. He was somehow able to clear the cobwebs from this brain sufficiently to realize that he was being guarded by only one person. Since he was lying motionless on his side facing the guard, with his eyes half-closed, the guard assumed that he was still unconscious. The guard thought this was especially so since he had kicked Robert in the ribs, and Robert did not cry out in pain. Robert watched the guard go inside the ship to see what was going on.

In spite of the pain in Robert's abdomen, his back, and his head, he was able to drag himself over to the starboard gunwale, and allow himself to fall five feet onto the ice below. This jarred his senses enough to realize that he had to get away from the ship as soon as he could. He basically crawled for one hundred yards in a direction that he perceived the commandos would not take on their return to their submarine. He then collapsed behind a hillock of ice.

When the men came back on the working deck and realized that Robert was gone, the commander was initially livid. Considering the darkness surrounding the ship, the commander decided that it would probably be fruitless to search for Robert. He ordered the men to get off the ship, and for the demolition experts to do their jobs. The commandos moved two hundred fifty yards away from the vessel, dragging their detonation wires behind them in the direction from which they had come. They got behind a low wall of ice, and detonated the plastic explosives. There were four sequential blasts, followed by a torch of a flame four to five hundred feet straight up into the area above the vessel. The flames were at least fifty feet in diameter. *Peary* sank beneath the ice within five minutes, and then there was total darkness where the vessel had once been.

From where Tom, Liz, and Mike were located, several miles from the ship, the explosion and the fireball were audible and visible. They were severely shaken by the sound and sight of the destruction of their ship, knowing full well that their friends and comrades were probably dead. Liz shouted, "We've got to go back. They may need our help!" Tom and Mike had to wrestle her to the ice to keep her from running back to see if anyone was still alive.

Tom said, as forcefully as he could without shouting, "Liz, this is why Robert wanted us to leave! You have to get hold of yourself, and realize that you would squander everything that he has done if we go back. His sacrifice might be wasted."

Although the shock of this event would probably not let them sleep, Tom decided that they should at least rest until it was lighter. Otherwise, he was afraid that one of them could be badly injured by a fall. As the austral dawn began to arrive, which by now was occurring around 8:00 AM, and the Russian commandos headed toward their pickup point with their submarine, the small group from *Peary* was startled to see a narrow ship slicing through the ice toward them. It was apparent that the ship had spotted them.

The commander of the Russian commandos did not know what to do. Their submarine lay directly ahead of them in the direction of the oncoming ship. Paralyzed by indecision, the seven commandos allowed themselves to be approached by the red and white vessel, which they recognized as the colors of the coast guards of all nations. Unfortunately for the Russians, the vessel flew the flag of the United States of America. The icebreaker encircled the commandos, cutting the ice in a circle around them, stranding the men on a large ice floe. The commandos did not have on their wetsuits, so there was no way for them to escape in the frigid water.

Having so put the Russians into an icy jail, the crew of the icebreaker launched a helicopter to search for survivors of the torched *Peary*. To the amazement of the pilots, they spotted a lone person near the large hole where the vessel had burned through the ice. When the chopper landed, they found that Robert's face and hands were severely frostbitten, and he was mumbling incoherently when they pulled him aboard. The crew chief on the chopper was finally able to understand that he was telling them that other people were on the ice in a direction of north-northeast, toward the Rothera research station.

The helicopter followed the directions given by Robert, and within ten minutes the crew spotted the yellow survival suits of Tom, Liz, and Mike. After picking them up, the helicopter crew headed back to the cutter. Robert appeared to be in shock. Liz tried to keep him warm by clinging to him during the flight. She constantly whispered something to him that no one else could hear over the chop-chop of the helicopter blades. Tom concluded that Robert probably had a ruptured spleen, and perhaps lacerations of the liver and pancreas from the blows to his abdomen. His kidneys had probably been damaged by the blows to his back. Just as the helicopter landed on the deck of the cutter, Robert died. Tom's efforts at resuscitation failed. Liz was inconsolable. Tom stared out across the ice and thought of one of his favorite quotes from Shakespeare: "Cowards die many times before their deaths. The valiant never taste of death but once." Mike went to the aft deck of the cutter, and wept alone.

The icebreaker picked up the Russian commandos, and secured them in the brig. In the meantime, two frigates of the Chilean Navy had arrived at the edge of the pack ice. Their sonar had detected the Russian sub for a few hours, and then they could no longer detect it. The captains of the two frigates felt confident that the American sub that had been following the Russian sub was once again on the Russian's tail, and that the U.S. Coast Guard icebreaker was safe. After a forty-eight-hour cruise, under an escort by the Chilean frigates, the icebreaker arrived at the U.S. research station at McMurdo Sound. The passengers aboard the icebreaker were loaded onto a waiting U.S. Air Force C-5A transport plane that had just landed with supplies and personnel for the austral summer.

During a refueling stop at a U.S. airbase in the Canal Zone, which was still being used as a base for the fifty-year-old U-2 spy planes, Tom and Mike surmised that these little planes might have been involved in the recent action involving *Byrd* and *Peary*. The C-5A then took *Byrd*'s the three surviving crew members to Dover Air Force Base in Delaware for handling of Robert's remains.

A team of CIA operatives took the seven Russians off to Langley, Virginia, for interrogation. After three months trapped in the Antarctic ice together, Tom, Liz, and Mike suddenly felt a great sense of emptiness instead of the joy that they had expected to feel. Their little family had been reduced to three, and they knew that they probably would never see each other again. Liz departed in a U.S. State Department limo accompanied by two well-dressed muscular and middle-aged men, whom Tom assumed would be escorting her back to the United Kingdom for debriefing at MI5 headquarters in London, before allowing her to go home to Scotland.

Tom and Mike were debriefed by two CIA agents in a hangar at Dover AFB, and then escorted to Ronald Reagan Washington National Airport for flights to New Orleans. From there, Mike went home to Bayou Lafourche, where *Byrd* and *Peary* had been built. As Tom reflected on the heroics of Robert and Chief, he thought of the lines of an old poem:

> The names of those who in their lives fought for life,
>
> Who wore at their hearts the fire's center,
>
> Born of the sun they traveled a short while towards the sun,
>
> And left the vivid air signed with their honor.
>
> From Stephen Spender,
> "I Think Continuously of Those Who Were Truly Great"